☑ KT-555-963

One Beastly Beast

Suffolk Schools Library Service

236514

For older readers

The Keys to the Kingdom

Mister Monday

Grim Tuesday

Drowned Wednesday

Sir Thursday

Lady Friday

SUFFOLK COUNTY COUNCIL SCHOOLS LIBRARY SERVICE	
236514	
30-May-2008	PETERS

GARTH NIX

One Beastly Beast

Two Aliens,
Three Inventors,
Four Fantastic Tales

Illustrated by Sholto Walker

HarperCollins *Children's Books*

To Stella Paskins, Ruth Katcher, Cathie Tasker and Kay Ronai,
the editors who brought these stories into print;
and as always, to Anna, Thomas and Edward

One Beastly Beast...
First published in in Great Britain by HarperCollins *Children's Books* 2007
HarperCollins *Children's Books* is a division of HarperCollins Publishers Ltd
77-85 Fulham Palace Road, Hammersmith, London, W6 8JB

Blackbread the Pirate Copyright © 1999 by Garth Nix. First published by Koala Books, Australia, 1999.
"The Princess and the Beastly Beast" Copyright © 2007 by Garth Nix. First published in *One Beastly Beast...*
HarperCollins *Children's Books*, 2007.
Bill the Inventor Copyright © 1998 by Garth Nix. First published by Koala Books, Australia, 1998.
Serena and the Sea Serpent Copyright © 2000 by Garth Nix. First published by Puffin, Penguin Books Australia, 2000.

www.harpercollinschildrensbooks.co.uk
www.garthnix.co.uk

4

One Beastly Beast... Copyright © Garth Nix 2007

ISBN 13: 978 0 00 723409 7
ISBN 10: 0 00 723409 0

The author and the illustrator assert the moral right to be identified as
the author and the illustrator of the work.

Printed and bound in Great Britain by
Clays Ltd, St Ives plc

Conditions of Sale
This book is sold subject to the condition that it shall not, by way of trade or otherwise,
be lent, re-sold, hired out or otherwise circulated without the publisher's prior written consent
in any form of binding or cover other than that in which it is published and without a similar
condition including this condition being imposed on the subsequent purchaser.

This book is proudly printed on paper which contains wood
from well managed forests, certified in accordance with
the rules of the Forest Stewardship Council.
For more information about FSC,
please visit www.fsc-uk.org

Contents

Blackbread the Pirate   9

The Princess and the Beastly Beast   65

Bill the Inventor   107

Serena and the Sea Serpent   161

Dear Reader,

Once upon a time, quite a long time ago, there was a boy who loved stories. He liked all kinds of stories, but particularly those about pirates, and aliens, and inventors, and sea serpents and knights and castles and monsters and dark nights when the moon was just a sliver in the sky, and a boy or a girl had to become a hero and take on terrible tasks to make everything right with the world.

The boy was lucky, because his parents loved stories too and their house was full of books, and he was even luckier still, because there was a library halfway between school and home. So he read more tales of adventure and excitement, more stories about talking animals and hideous beasts and brave children and magic both fair and foul.

That boy, of course, was me. I still love all kinds of stories, but most of all I like the ones that tell of fantastic creatures and fabulous places. When I grew up, I found out that I didn't want to just read stories like that, I wanted to write them.

I've pretty much written all my books for myself. When I write, I just try to tell the kind of story that I like to read. These four stories in particular are for that young boy, who more than thirty-five years ago signed up for a life of adventure through reading.

Garth Nix

Blackbread
the Pirate

Chapter One

"Take these videos back to the shop, please," said Peter's mum. She took two DVDs out of her shopping bag and handed them to her son. "They have to be back by two o'clock or they cost extra."

"OK," said Peter. Anything to get away from the boredom of following his mother around. "Which video shop, Mum?"

"VideoPleaseMe," said Mum as she locked the car. "Right over there. Then come straight over to the supermarket."

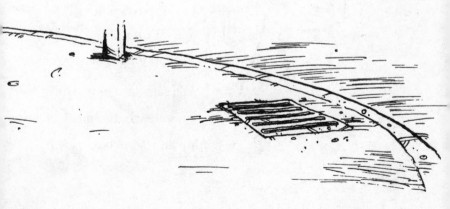

"Yes, Mum," said Peter, rolling his eyes. Anyone would think he was still a little kid.

"And no, you can't have any money to rent games for your PlayStation," added Mum as Peter opened his mouth.

"Yes, Mum," said Peter.

Peter trudged over to the shop, pretending that he was slow-marching in a procession. He held the two DVDs out in front of him like some sort of ceremonial regalia. *The sacred DVDs of the king,* he thought, and laughed.

"Make way for the king's DVDs," he said in a mock-regal voice to no one in particular as he crossed the car park.

"King's DVDs!" said a voice from somewhere ahead of him and somehow down below.

Peter stopped pretending to be the king and tried to see who was talking. But there was no one around. Just one lady getting into her car. Besides, the voice sounded low and gruff. It couldn't have come from her.

"Down here, matey!"

It was louder now. A deep and somehow slightly nasty voice that made Peter think of running away. But he took a quick, deep breath instead… and looked down.

Chapter Two

Just in front of Peter's feet there was a heavy steel grating set in the ground – a kind of manhole for the drains – and that's where the voice was coming from.

"What are you doing in the drain?" asked Peter. His voice quavered a bit, though he was more surprised than frightened.

"Ar, that'd be a tale to tell," answered the voice. "A tale as wot's longer than my tail, if yer take my meaning."

Peter didn't take his meaning, but he knelt down to take a closer look, putting the videos on the ground next to the grating. But as soon as he let go of them, the grating suddenly moved up and sideways. Peter instinctively jumped back. Then he stood and stared, unable to believe what he was seeing.

Four enormous black rats jumped out of the drain – rats that stood on their hind legs and came up as far as his knees. But these weren't just really big rats. They had clothes on, old-fashioned clothes with big wide belts and floppy hats. Three of them held cutlasses in their pink paws, and one was pointing two pistols at Peter. Old pistols like the kind that humans hadn't used for more than a hundred years, but rat-sized.

"You're pirates!" exclaimed Peter, taking in additional details such as the eyepatch on the biggest, meanest-looking rat, and the skull and crossbones dyed white on his black chest fur, where his red shirt was rudely unbuttoned to the waist.

"Yes, we be pirates!" growled the rat with the eyepatch, gesturing to his mates to pick up the two DVDs. "We be video pirates, ah har, and those there discs will fetch us a pretty sum. I advise yer to step aside, lad, if yer knows wot's good for yer!"

"But video pirates just copy stuff," said Peter frowning. "They don't steal them! We'll have to pay a fine if you steal our DVDs."

"Don't tell us how to do our piratin'," said the rat menacingly. "We're taking these here DVDs and that's that!"

Quickly, the rats passed the DVDs down into the drain,

while the one with the eyepatch kept his pistols trained on Peter. After the others had climbed back down, this last rat hesitated, then raised his pistols.

"Don't try and follow us!" he ordered. "And don't go blabbing to the navy, neither."

With that said, he carefully uncocked the pistols and thrust them through his belt, before diving after his gang. Judging from the rat's caution with the guns, Peter got the impression that he'd probably once had a nasty accident with them.

He was just bending over to look down the drain when the pirate rat suddenly popped back up, teeth shining evilly in the sun.

"Don't even think about following us!" he snarled, before disappearing again.

Peter stood absolutely still for a minute and

listened carefully. He could hear distant echoes coming from the drain, as if the rats were singing as they marched away. Away with his DVDs. Peter felt half angry and half petrified, but mostly he thought, *What can I say to Mum? Four pirate rats stole the DVDs and I didn't do anything?*

He took a step forward, and then another. His foot was in the air for the third and final step when the mean-looking rat popped out again.

"I said—" he started to say, then his eyes bulged, his whiskers sprang out absolutely straight and he ducked back down into the drain.

Chapter Three

"Halt in the name of the king!" shouted a voice behind Peter. Before he could turn round to look, more rats raced past him. They were the same size as the pirates, but these were wearing blue-and-white-striped shirts and red cloth caps, and they all had pistols as well as cutlasses. They quickly surrounded the drainhole, ignoring Peter, except for the rat who was obviously their leader.

"Ruffians!" exclaimed this important-looking rat, and marched over to Peter. Peter looked down at him, taking in the blue uniform with gold buttons and braid, and the shiny black arched hat.

"I guess you're the navy," said Peter slowly. He couldn't think of anything else to say.

"Well done, sir," exclaimed the rat. "Captain Erasmus Rattus at your service, of His Majesty's Royal Ratship *Tumblewheel*. Currently on an anti-piracy cruise."

"They took my DVDs," said Peter. "Four horrible pirates! One had an eyepatch."

"The scurvy knaves!" exclaimed Captain Rattus angrily. "If coming up Topside ain't bad enough, it's pirating videos as well. What's your name, lad?"

"Peter," said Peter.

"A goodly name," said the captain. "Like the Blue Peter flag we fly when we're leaving port. That's a name for adventure, that is. I expect you'll be wanting to come with us to recover your cargo?"

"Cargo?" asked Peter. "What cargo?"

"The DVDs!" cried Captain Rattus. "Why, if we don't catch those pirates soon, they'll be turning those DVDs into Frisbees and earrings and coasters and trading them for gold and ivory. They're probably almost back to their ship by now. Are you coming with us?"

He pointed at the open drain and the sailor rats started to jump down, one after the other. Soon there was only the captain and Peter left. Peter looked at the hole and thought of the lost DVDs.

"I'm too big to get down there," he said finally. He didn't know if he wanted to go or not. He did like the sound of an adventure, but he wasn't sure about all these rats.

"Too big?" muttered Captain Rattus. "We'll soon fix that. Where's the doctor!"

"Here, sir!" piped up a rat Peter hadn't even noticed. An unobtrusive rat in a scruffy brown coat, who was lurking way back near another drain. He hurried over, pulled out a monocle, stuck it in his eye and peered up at Peter.

"Doctor Abednego Norvegicus at your service," he said. "I take it that this is a matter of shrinkage, captain?"

"Shrinking!" corrected the captain. "Peter here wants to sign on for the duration."

"Oh, I'm not sure if that's exactly—" said Peter anxiously. "The duration" sounded like a very long time.

"Well, as long as it takes to recover his cargo or when he gets sick of it then," said the captain. "So if you could please shrink him down immediately, doctor, that would be most agreeable."

"Hmmm," said the doctor, looking up at Peter and making estimating motions with his arms. "How old are you, Peter?"

"Nine," said Peter. "In July."

"Very well," said the doctor. "Since I haven't a potion or the necessary lotion in the quantities you would require, it will have to be a spell."

Chapter Four

"A spell?" asked the captain. His nose twitched and he muttered, "Mumbo jumbo hocus pocus—"

"Not that spell, Captain!" exclaimed the doctor, raising one pink paw in protest.

"I didn't know *that* was a spell," said the captain. "I'll just nip down this hole while you get on with it."

He'd no sooner finished speaking than he was gone, his magnificently long tail trailing behind him for a full half-second.

"Is this shrinking spell dangerous?" asked Peter, who was having second thoughts about the whole adventure. "Maybe I should just tell Mum I lost the DVDs…"

"It's not dangerous at all," said the doctor soothingly, as he rummaged in his waistcoat for a piece of chalk. Having found it, he quickly inscribed some magic marks on Peter's white trainers.

Since the chalk was white too, Peter couldn't see the marks, but the doctor seemed satisfied.

"Now, I shall utter the spell," said the doctor. He reached up over his head as if he were pegging out washing. "You may want to close your eyes, Peter. Being shrunk sometimes makes people vomit if they look."

Peter nodded, but he didn't shut his eyes. He was never sick, not even on the Planet Freefall ride at the Easter Show, which everyone called the Chucker-Upper.

The doctor started making strange motions with his paws, then began to dance anticlockwise around Peter, stopping every few steps to stamp his feet.

"Widdershins, widdershins, baker's man *(stomp stomp)*
Make this boy as small as you can *(stomp stomp)*
But like the dough that makes the bread *(stomp stomp)*
He'll rise again when the words are said!" *(stomp stomp)*

The doctor finished with a surprising triple spin that sent his tail whipping round in a circle. Then he lowered his arms as if he were trying to drag Peter down without actually touching him.

At first, the boy felt nothing; then the whole world went blurry and everything started to twist and roll around him. He felt himself shrinking, the cars growing taller and taller around him. The doctor loomed up past his waist, past his shoulders, and then the rat was standing right next to him and they were exactly the same size.

"You didn't throw up," said Doctor Norvegicus. He sounded surprised and disappointed.

"Mmppphhh," said Peter, who was doing his best not to be sick after all.

"Ah, all rat-sized, shipshape and Bristol fashion!" declared the captain, poking his nose out of the drain. "Let's get below!"

Chapter Five

Still holding his mouth closed, Peter followed the doctor to the drain. He'd expected it to be just a small concrete tunnel full of water, but there was actually a very deep hole and a rope ladder that descended into darkness. The captain was standing on one of the upper rungs, consulting a pocket chronometer and a thick book with very thin pages.

"Look sharp!" he ordered. "This hole will close in a few minutes."

Without waiting, the captain started down. Peter and the doctor followed quickly. It wasn't until they were about fifty rungs down that Peter felt better and dared to open his mouth.

"Where are we going?" he asked. "And what do you mean, this hole will close?"

"We're going back to the Neverworld," replied the captain easily, not at all out of breath from climbing, despite his heavy coat and sword. "That's where we come from. Sometimes holes poke through from the Neverworld to your world and people cross over. There are books that predict where these world-holes will appear. Interworld almanacs – like the one you just saw me use. But these pirates have managed to get their hands on something even more useful, I'm afraid."

"An orrery," said the doctor.

"What's a... what you said?" asked Peter.

"Mostly it's pricklesome hard to pronounce," replied the captain. "*Oh-rair-ree*. See what I mean?"

"An orrery is usually a model of how the planets move around the sun," explained the doctor, ignoring Captain Rattus. "But there were some special sorcerous orreries made by the famous magician Leonardo Ratinci several hundred years ago. A Ratinci's

orrery can show you where all the holes between the worlds are and when they will be."

"Those detestable pirates stole a Ratinci orrery from a rich merchant," explained the captain. "We've been following them for days, trying to get it back. If we don't, they'll pop up all over your world and do their evil business, stealing DVDs and suchlike."

"I see," said Peter, beginning to understand the situation. Mostly he wanted to get his own DVDs back, but clearly a Ratinci orrery shouldn't be left in the hands of pirates. Thinking of his own DVDs made him realise he couldn't possibly deliver them before two o'clock or get back before his mother finished shopping.

"Oh," he said, stopping. "I've just realised that I have to go back. My mum'll miss me."

"No, no," cried the doctor. "Keep on! The world-hole is closing above us!"

Chapter Six

Peter looked up, and sure enough the sides of the hole were flowing inwards like mud into a bottle. Quickly, he started down again, almost slipping on the next few rungs.

"In any case," puffed the doctor below him, "you won't be missed. Time is different in the Neverworld. In fact, if you stay here too long, you might end up going back before you left. Or if you choose the wrong hole between the Neverworld and Topside – which is what we call where you come from – you might end up going back years before you were even born."

Peter didn't like the sound of that at all. He was already regretting coming on this adventure. He was tired of this rope ladder that seemed to descend for a kilometre at least through the gloomy, dismal darkness. Besides, there was no knowing what was at the other end of this world-hole. Maybe the doctor and the captain were lying and they were taking him away to be a slave, and he'd never see the sun again, or his mum, or anything.

"Don't worry," said the doctor, who seemed to know what he was feeling. "We'll send you back safely. And we're nearly there. Look down."

Peter looked and saw a bright light shining up past the two rats below him on the ladder. It looked like sunshine, though that didn't seem possible.

But it *was* sunshine. Peter blinked as he came out and the sun's rays hit him in the face. When he stopped blinking, he saw that he was hanging on a rope ladder that was invisibly attached to the air. Above there was a

blue sky with a few lazy white clouds bumbling along.
Below him, there was a clump of palm trees and a golden
beach.

Looking around, Peter saw that he was on an island.
Anchored not far from shore, there was a ship with white
sails and lots of red-capped sailors climbing over its masts
and rigging. On the other side of the island, another ship
with all its putrid yellow sails set was sailing away as fast
as it could.

"There go the villains!" shouted the captain, jumping to the ground. "Quick! To the *Tumblewheel!*"

A few minutes later, Peter was on board His Majesty's Royal Rat Ship *Tumblewheel*. He was out of breath from running and soaked from wading into the surf to get picked up by one of the ship's small boats. There were rat sailors running all around him, climbing up the rigging, raising sails, tying and untying ropes, hauling on ropes and turning the windlass that raised the anchor. Captain Rattus was already on the poop deck, shouting orders as the ship slowly started to turn out to sea, the wind filling its sails and all the timbers and ropes groaning as if the *Tumblewheel* was reluctant to move.

"Mister Purser!" shouted the captain, pointing at Peter. "We've a gentleman volunteer aboard that needs a proper rig-out. See to it, if you please."

A small, older-looking rat appeared at Peter's elbow and led him away below deck. It was surprisingly cramped and Peter had to duck his head as they clambered down steps and through doorways and hatches. It smelled too, of salt and wet rats.

"Here we go, sir," said the purser finally, as they

reached a small room full of chests and bags. "We'll have you kitted out in a moment. Hoi, Patrick! Get Mister…"

"Peter," said Peter.

"Get Mister Peter a cutlass and a brace of pistols from Hodges the Armourer," ordered the purser. Then he took a deep breath and started to hand Peter clothing, reciting, "Here's a blue coat of best superfine with one inch brass buttons on a nautical line; a linen shirt somewhat patched with a detachable collar that's practically a match; a pair of double-seated britches made of wool that sadly itches; two pairs of stockings, one silk, one not; a pair of sea boots with holes where they've been shot; a broad leather belt with steel buckle showing faint remains of gilt; and a broad-brimmed hat of salt-stained felt."

A few minutes later, Peter had changed into his new clothes and was realising the truth of the purser's words. The double-seated breeches did itch. Still, he couldn't help but stick his chest out and feel proud in his seagoing gear. Then Able Searat Patrick came back with a cutlass and a brace of pistols, which Peter was relieved to see meant only two.

"Captain says I'm to show you how to shoot," said Patrick. "Because we'll be boarding those rotten rascal pirates within the hour. And I'll teach you a few cutlass tricks as well."

Chapter Seven

Peter followed Patrick out of the hold from the purser's office to the gun deck, weaving between the rats who were waiting beside the great brass cannons. Past the last cannon, they climbed up a ladder and through a hatch.

Out in the open air, Patrick showed Peter how to fire his pistols and hold his cutlass. Peter shot at a floating barrel and learned how to reload; then he put the pistols away to hack at a spar with the cutlass and learn the basics of attack and defence.

"We're… we're not going to get killed, are we?" he asked Patrick nervously. Half an hour of practice with the pistols and cutlass had shown him how dangerous they could be.

"Of course not!" said Patrick, surprise in his bright black eyes. "This is the Neverworld! You only get awfully wounded here and suffer terrible pain till you get better or grow back a paw or tail. No one dies."

"Terrible pain?" asked Peter faintly. "I don't like the sound of that!"

"Patrick always exaggerates," said a small, balding rat who was sharpening his cutlass nearby. "It ain't that bad. Why, I've had both my ears shot off and I hardly noticed when it happened. The doc gave me a cordial and they grew back in two weeks, though I've had a little trouble with my fur."

"Oh," said Peter. "Things are very different where I come from."

"Naturally," said the balding rat. "That's Topside. All sorts of strange things happen there. You just stick with the captain, Mister Peter. He'll see you through."

"Speaking of the captain," said Patrick, "I think he wants you on the poop."

"The poop?"

"The deck at the back, where the captain paces to and fro, grappling with strategies and tactics and cunning plans to defeat the foe," explained the purser, who had just come on deck. "How are the britches?"

"They itches," said Peter as he climbed the short ladder to the poop deck. The captain was looking through a telescope, but he clapped it shut and shook Peter's hand with one powerful paw.

"It's good to see a fellow take to this way of life," he declared. "Are your pistols primed and ready? Cutlass sharp as it can get?"

"Yes, sir," declared Peter, who suddenly felt braver for the captain's handshake.

"Hmm," said the captain, as if he wasn't sure what to say next. He took Peter's arm and led him away from the two rats who stood nearby at the ship's wheel.

"There's a bit of a problem," he whispered. "I've recognised the pirate ship and the news is not good. You see, we can't risk destroying the Ratinci orrery by sinking the ship with cannon fire, so we'll have to board and fight it out. But that ship's the *Nasty Cupboard* and its captain is none other than—"

He looked around to make sure no one was listening, then pushed his snout so close to Peter's ear that his whiskers tickled the boy's cheek.

"Its captain… its captain is none other than the worst pirate who ever sailed the seas. The most awful bandit of the oceans, the most ghastly robber of the deep. A rat whose true name cannot be spoken, a rat who is only known by the fearsome weapon he employs, the rat that we call—"

"I say," interrupted Doctor Norvegicus loudly as he climbed up to the poop deck. He peered through his monocle at the pirate ship. "Isn't that the *Nasty Cupboard?* The ship captained by the most awful pirate of our times, the villainous, terrible, disgusting, horrendous rat who is known only as—"

"Blackbread," finished Captain Rattus, giving up on whispering. As the name echoed out, the fur on the rats across the deck paled from black to grey and their tails began to shiver.

"Blackbread?" asked Peter. "Why is he called that?"

"He has a magic weapon," explained the doctor. "A long thin loaf of ancient petrified black bread. It's harder than iron and sharper than a diamond, and its magic powers make Blackbread entirely bulletproof. They bounce off the loaf and off him as well. Some have tried to fight him using only

sword or cutlass, but he is too dangerous for that. Blackbread is a true master of the loaf."

"There's not a rat aboard the *Tumblewheel* that dares to face Blackbread," sighed Captain Rattus. "Including, I'm sad to say, myself. We'll just have to let him go."

Chapter Eight

"But what about my DVDs! And the Ratinci orrery!" exclaimed Peter. "We have to get them back!"

"I'm sorry, Peter," said the captain, and a tear glistened in his eye. "We dare not risk Blackbread's anger, not even for the orrery... or your DVDs. Helmsrat, hard aport!"

The crew cheered as the *Tumblewheel* turned aside. Then they groaned as the *Nasty Cupboard* turned as well and continued sailing towards them.

"The hunter becomes the hunted," said the doctor, peering through his monocle at the pirate ship. "We'll have to fight Blackbread after all."

"What would happen if Blackbread lost his loaf?" asked Peter, who'd been thinking very hard about the situation. It seemed to him that the navy rats had given up too easily.

"Why, he'd be nothing," said Captain Rattus. "Just another bad rat to be taken in for justice. But he carries the loaf by night and day. It's impossible! We're all going to be taken as prisoners and sold as slaves!"

"I was thinking that if you carried something sort of soft and sticky as a shield, Blackbread might get his loaf stuck in it," said Peter. "Then you could wrestle with him and take the loaf away."

"Wrestle with him?" squeaked the captain. "He's the biggest rat around! And we haven't got a soft and sticky shield."

"The boy's right!" exclaimed the doctor, hopping up and down with excitement. "Why didn't we think of it before? Our champion can use the ship's cheese to trap the loaf. Bread and cheese go together like… like rats and whiskers. The loaf will throw itself at the cheese, whether Blackbread wants it to or not."

"But that cheese weighs a ton. We had to get it aboard with a crane," said the captain, pointing to a huge round of cheese that was lashed to the deck for safety and easy nibbling. "The legendary Ratercules could lift it and maybe wrestle with Blackbread, but no one here is big enough, or strong enough, or brave enough."

"Maybe not right this second," said Peter. "Doctor Norvegicus – when you put the spell on me, you said I'd rise like dough when words were said. Can you say just one or two of the words to make me grow bigger, but not so big that I can't fit through the hole to Topside?"

"There's seven magic words to say for you to regain your proper height," mused the doctor. "I think three of them would make you a giant here, yet not so big you couldn't get back home. I'm not entirely sure. But even if I make you big enough and strong enough, are you brave enough?"

"Considering," the captain interrupted, "that if you

don't fight Blackbread we'll all be taken prisoner and sold as slaves, to work in the Barbary video shops, shining discs until our paws are rubbed to stumps."

Peter gulped and rubbed his stomach, trying to get rid of the sick feeling in his middle. What if his plan failed and he was cut to pieces by the loaf? Patrick had said he wouldn't die, but it would hurt worse that anything, and even when he got better he'd be a slave. But if he didn't try, there wasn't any chance at all.

"I'll do it," he said.

Chapter Nine

The captain stared at Peter, a small tear forming in his right eye. "You're a brave boy," he said. "Whatever happens, it's been an honour to sail with you."

"Likewise," said the doctor. "An honour."

Both rats saluted. Peter nodded. Then the three of them turned to look at the approaching enemy.

The *Nasty Cupboard* was sailing fast towards the *Tumbleweed*. Hundreds of pirates hung off the rigging and stood along the deck, all of them laughing and shouting threats. On the poop deck, one rat stood alone. A huge black rat with pink eyes, wearing a coat the colour of old compost. In his hand he held a long loaf of petrified black bread that seemed to cast a cloud of darkness all around him, despite the summer sun.

It could only be Blackbread. As Peter watched, he raised the sharp stick of bread and bellowed, "Run 'em down and board 'em, and I'll make 'em meet the loaf!"

Rats screamed, the helmsrat let go of the wheel, and the *Tumblewheel* turned into the wind and stopped dead in the water. A few seconds later, the two ships crashed into each other with the sound of shrieking wood and shouting rats.

In those two seconds, Doctor Norvegicus whispered in Peter's ear, "Hic haec hoc."

Peter's eyes went blurry, the world melted around him and he felt himself stretching out. In the first second he was half as tall as the doctor, and then the doctor was only as high as his waist.

"Quick! Undo the cheese!" shouted Peter.

His voice was so loud that it blew the doctor's hat off and it shut up all the screaming sailors. Both ships fell silent as Blackbread jumped on to the deck of the *Tumblewheel*.

He waved the gleaming black loaf above his head and cried, "A Topside champion? You dare to face Blackbread?"

"Yes!" cried Peter. He grabbed a rope, swung down to the cheese and lifted the huge round over his own head. But before he could throw it, Blackbread darted forward, thrusting the terrible loaf straight at Peter's guts.

Peter sucked in his stomach and the point of the loaf whistled through the air. Blackbread spat upon the deck and pulled the loaf back for another stab.

"You're not much of a hero," he sneered, and he laughed a particularly evil laugh.

But Blackbread's laugh faltered as the loaf in his hand suddenly twitched and wriggled of its own accord. The pirate's bushy eyebrows rose in surprise as his paw jerked forward and jiggled from side to side as if the loaf was trying to hurl itself at the cheese.

Peter held his breath, partly because he was so excited but also because the cheese really stank. It looked like his plan was going to work!

"Stop!" screamed Blackbread. He gripped the loaf with both paws and even wrapped his tail around it. But the fearsome bread slowly inched itself out of his grasp.

"Nooooo!" howled Blackbread. His paws grappled with the air as the loaf launched itself at the cheese like a rocket. It struck so hard that it almost completely disappeared, only the end of its blackened crust still visible.

Quick as a flash, Peter threw the cheese and loaf into the sea. The round bobbed up once like a giant cork, then sank, the bright yellow of the cheese disappearing into the dark blue of the ocean's depths.

Chapter Ten

"I've lost my loaf," said Blackbread, and he sat down on the deck and started to cry. His crew, who moments before had been the fiercest pirates afloat, started to blubber as well. Soon the entire crew of the *Nasty Cupboard* were weeping and gnashing their teeth. They didn't stop wailing or offer any resistance even as they were put in chains for the voyage back to port.

While the pirates were being chained up, other rats searched the *Nasty Cupboard* for the stolen DVDs. Doctor Norvegicus went too, to try and find the Ratinci orrery.

"Well done, Peter," said Captain Rattus. "Quick thinking and brave to boot! If you ever want to make the Royal Rat

Navy your career, you need only say the word."

"Wouldn't I have to be a rat?" asked Peter.

"A technicality," replied the captain, waving a paw. "Besides, I'm sure the doctor could turn you into one. Would you like to give it a try? It's really quite excellent, I assure you. A nice furry body, a tail to balance with, fantastic teeth—"

"No, no thank you," interrupted Peter. "I really should be getting back as soon as I can."

"Pointy ears," continued the captain. He took off his hat to show how he could turn and tilt his own fine ears.

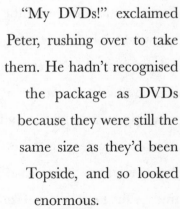

"Ah, there's the doctor back, and a couple of the lads with some loot... I mean reclaimed cargo."

"My DVDs!" exclaimed Peter, rushing over to take them. He hadn't recognised the package as DVDs because they were still the same size as they'd been Topside, and so looked enormous.

"I have the Ratinci orrery," exclaimed the doctor, putting a box down on the deck. "Take a look in here, Peter."

Norvegicus pointed at a small brass-rimmed peephole in the top of the box. Peter looked in.

At first, all he could see was a white mist. But it slowly cleared and he saw that the box contained an amazingly beautiful globe made of gold and silver wire. All the countries of the Neverworld were there, and Peter saw that he could concentrate on just one country and it would grow bigger and bigger, and if he kept looking, it would focus on a single village or even a house or a clump of trees. And sometimes there would be a glowing spot next to the trees or the house or the lake, and silvery letters would spell

out a time and date and other numbers and letters that he didn't understand.

"It's fantastic!" cried Peter. "It's showing where all the holes are through to my world, isn't it?

"And other worlds," said Doctor Norvegicus. "I have already used it to find a world-hole to send you home. It'll take you back to where we met, only a few minutes after we left."

"Oh," said Peter. "Couldn't I stay longer and still get

back in time? I'm enjoying my adventure now we've got Blackbread all chained up."

He glanced over at the still blubbering pirate captain, who was now almost hidden under his wrapping of many chains.

"I'm afraid you have to go now, Peter," said the doctor. "There are only a few world-holes suitable so we should use the closest one while we can. You still have one small adventure left though."

"I do?" asked Peter.

"Yes," said the doctor, smiling. "The hole isn't on land. So we will have to climb the mast to get to it and jump to the rope ladder."

Peter looked up at the mast towering over him and gulped. It seemed very, very high, and with the rocking of the ship, the mast moved a lot from side to side.

"Are you coming with me?" he asked. He didn't like the thought of climbing up so high alone, and then having to jump...

"Indeed I am," said the doctor. "I'd better grow your old clothes a bit so you can get changed. We'll have to climb soon. Captain, if I could have a word about the course?"

"Certainly," replied the captain. "May I say once again, young Peter, that it has been an honour to sail with you. May we meet again!"

"Thank you," said Peter.

"Three cheers for the young gentleman!" shouted the captain. He threw his hat in the air and the cheers of the rats echoed across the water as Peter went below to get changed.

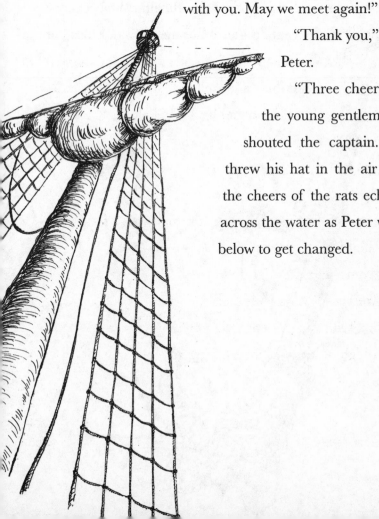

Chapter Eleven

All too soon, Peter found himself clinging to the very top of the mast, with the DVDs strapped to his back and the doctor hanging on beneath him. The sea was fairly calm, but even so, the mast did swing at least ten metres from side to side, and the ship and the sea looked very small and far away below them.

They had already missed the world-hole on their first attempt, with the ship passing the spot a little too far away. This time it looked like they were perfectly aligned. Peter could see and almost touch the rope ladder that hung just below the hole, which looked like a strange circle of darkness in the sky. But with the ship going up and down the waves, and the mast going sideways as the ship rolled, he was really afraid to jump.

"Never fear!" shouted the doctor below him. The rat's voice was hard to hear over the wind and the groaning of the mast and the rigging. Peter nodded and gulped, his eyes fixed on the dangling ladder. The ship drew closer and closer and he steeled himself to jump.

"Five... four... three... two... JUMP!" shouted the doctor, and Peter jumped, his arms thrashing ahead of him in a desperate effort to grab hold of the ladder.

For a horrible instant he thought he'd missed it; then his hands hit something and he gripped hard and hung on for dear life. The ship kept going as Peter swung on the ladder from the sky, a few rungs from the bottom.

All the rats cheered and the captain saluted, but Peter didn't see him – he had his eyes shut tight. It wasn't until the doctor tapped him on the foot that he opened them again and saw that the rat was only just hanging on by his paws from the very last rung of the rope ladder.

"Be a good boy and start climbing, would you?" asked the doctor nicely.

"Sorry," mumbled Peter, and started to climb. Only then did he think to ask about how Doctor Norvegicus would get back, since he couldn't imagine trying to jump from this world-hole to the mast of the *Tumblewheel*.

"Oh, I'm not going back the same way!" explained the doctor. He turned his body so Peter could see that he had the Ratinci orrery strapped to his back. "I'll use the orrery to find another world-hole."

They climbed in silence. From time to time Peter scraped his shoulders on the sides of the hole, which was a weird feeling since it felt both hard like a brick wall and soft like a deep carpet. But the doctor had judged his size well. Soon Peter saw sunlight filtering down through some bars above and knew he was about to return to his own world.

Carefully, he pushed the grating open and climbed out… but not into the lane next to the supermarket. For a second he felt a terrible fear that he'd ended up in the wrong place and maybe even the wrong time.

Then he realised that he was on the other side of the supermarket, on the edge of the car park. It seemed to be the right time of day, as far as he could tell.

"I'll say goodbye here," said Doctor Norvegicus. "And I'd also better say yan, tan, tethera, methera."

With those four words spoken, Peter suddenly grew up to his normal height. When his eyes stopped being blurry, and he was sure he wasn't going to be sick, he looked down. The doctor was gone and there was only a shallow drain under the metal grating.

Shaking his head, Peter walked around to the video shop and handed over the DVDs. After that he wondered over to the supermarket, kicking the ground and wondering if any of his strange adventure had actually happened. Had he somehow fallen asleep and dreamed the whole thing?

He was still wondering when he tripped over the mat at the supermarket door. Something fell out of his pocket and rolled across the floor as he got up. Peter caught it before it went under the trolleys and stared at it. It was a coin. A large and very heavy gold coin that showed a crowned rat on one side and a coat of arms on the other. It said *Rattus Rex Imp NV* around the figure of the crowned rat and *Defender of the Rodents* around the coat of arms. Peter laughed and put the coin back in his pocket. It might come in handy if he ever went back to the Neverworld.

"That was quick," said his mum absently when he joined her at the checkout. As she waited for her change, she looked at Peter more carefully.

"It's strange," she said. "You seem taller somehow and sort of more tanned. But you've only been gone five minutes."

"Yes, Mum," said Peter, with a small and secret smile.

The Princess
and the
Beastly Beast

Chapter One

"There is a beastly beast on the battlements," said Princess Chlorinda. "A bloody beastly beast."

"You mustn't swear, Rinda," said Queen Alba absently. She was sitting at her grand piano and didn't even look at her daughter. She was too busy composing an opera. She had been a full-time warrior maiden before her marriage, and a part-time one afterwards, but she had recently packed away her weapons and armour and taken up music composition instead. Just for a few years, until it was time to start training Rinda to be a warrior maiden too.

Being a composer meant the queen hummed to herself a lot and spent hours and hours at the piano.

"I'm not swearing," Rinda explained. "It *is* a bloody beastly beast. It's covered in blood. I expect from its gruesome and ghastly habits."

"Well, tell the guard," said the queen, waving with one hand as she tapped out a few notes with the other. "I'm at a tricky part."

"You're always at a tricky part," complained Rinda. "And the guard has locked himself in his barracks and says he won't come out."

"Well, tell your father," said the queen. "He can deal with a bloody beastly beast."

"If it eats me it will be your fault!" protested Rinda.

"The trick is to get past the teeth in one leap and go straight down the gullet," instructed the queen, to the accompaniment of a

few dramatic chords from her latest composition. "Then you can cut your way free from the inside."

"You're disgusting!" shouted Rinda as she stormed out of the room.

The queen sighed and thought about going after her. But Rinda was always making up stories of monsters and beasties and black-hearted dwarves who travelled in company with dragons.

Outside the queen's tower, Rinda stopped to check that the bloody beastly beast was still on the battlements. It was, sitting quite contentedly above the main gate. Rinda frowned and stalked across the courtyard to her father's tower.

It only took a minute as they lived in a very small castle. There was the Queen's Tower, the King's Tower, the Princess's Tower (smaller than the other two), the Guard's Barracks (which was a pleasant whitewashed cottage in the courtyard), and the kitchy-store-cellar-thingy, which was a ramshackle house with lots of funny little rooms and a large kitchen. It was wedged between the King's and Queen's Towers and half of it stuck out through the castle walls.

Rinda's frown set deeper into her forehead as she saw that her father had shut the door to his tower and the key wasn't in the lock. She threw herself at the solid oak door like a battering ram and hammered with her fists.

"Let me in! Let me in! There's a bloody beastly beast on the battlements!"

Chapter Two

After a few minutes hammering, the door swung open and Rinda fell inside. No one had opened the door, but this didn't surprise Rinda. Her father, as well as being the king, was a wizard. His tower supposedly had an invisible servant, who opened doors and made tea and washed the floor. A year ago Rinda had thrown flour in the air to see what the invisible servant looked like and had been very disappointed. The invisible servant looked exactly like her father. He'd sneezed and run away, and then had come back visible, pretending that he wasn't the invisible servant after all.

"Dad!" shouted Rinda. "I know you opened the door."

The air shimmered in front of her and her father appeared. King Victor was very tall and thin. He wore a wizard's robe adorned with silver stars. That was even taller than he was, so it dragged on the ground and he often tripped over it. It was a bit chilly in his tower so he was also wearing a comfy red cardigan that was missing a few buttons. Both robe and cardigan were a little stained from spilled potions and burned at the edges from misfired spells.

"What is it, Chlorinda?" the king asked. "I'm very busy extracting essence of dragon from a dragon's tooth."

"There's a bloody beastly beast on the battlements," said Rinda.

"Don't swear—" her father started to say. Then he saw Rinda's frown deepen even more and he caught on. "Oh, you mean it is bloody, as in actually bloody. In that it has blood upon it. Is it dripping or just a sort of stain?"

"Dripping, in bucketloads," confirmed Rinda. "Mother won't deal with it and the guard won't come out, so you'll have to."

"Shouldn't you be at school?" countered the king.

Rinda rolled her eyes. Didn't anyone ever pay attention to what she was saying?

"It's summer break," she said. "It started three days ago! I'm supposed to be on holiday, but I'm not having any fun. And there's a bloody beastly beast—"

"Yes, yes, I know, on the battlements. Look, Rinda, I really am very busy. Why don't you come back at lunchtime and we'll take a look at this beast together? See it off with a few jumping sparks or a spot of agonising ointment?"

"It might eat me for its lunchtime first," said Rinda darkly.

"If it does, the trick is to get past its teeth in one leap and go straight down its gullet," said the king. "Your mother's done it once or twice—"

But he was talking to empty air. Rinda had run outside. The king sighed and thought about going after her. But Rinda was always making up stories about ghastly ghosts and toothy termagants. So he turned himself invisible and shut the door, for a king cannot be seen to shut his own doors.

Chapter Three

Rinda stalked angrily away from her father's tower and went to sit on the battlements with the bloody beastly beast. It was actually her pet pig, Horace, that she'd covered with strawberry jam. Horace had managed to lick his legs and the front half of himself free of jam, but he couldn't reach the jam on his back. He kept squealing and chasing his curly tail in an effort to get to the last bits of sweet strawberry.

"Stop that, Horace!" commanded Rinda, but the pig paid her no attention.

Rinda stared out across the lands beyond the castle as Horace chased himself round in a circle. The lands beyond weren't very interesting. Across the moat and up the road there was a small shallow river with a short narrow bridge across it. Rinda had hoped a troll might move in under the bridge, but so far none had. There were several farmhouses inhabited by cheery farmers, none of whom appeared to be werewolves. There were fields of crops, all boring stuff like wheat and barley, without a screaming mandrake root anywhere. There were cows, none of them with two heads or flaming eyes. There were sheep, which were just... sheep.

"It's boring here and everyone hates me," said Rinda. "I'm going to run away and have an adventure."

Horace grunted, which was not the encouragement Rinda had hoped for.

"I am going to run away," Rinda repeated. "Right now!"

"I really am going to run away!" shouted Rinda. She was hoping that someone else might hear. But no one paid her any attention. Not even Horace. He'd finally managed to get some more jam into his mouth.

Rinda looked over the wall. It was supposed to be twelve feet high, but only the back wall of the castle had actually been finished properly. Here the wall was just a few feet taller than she was.

"I'm running away right now!" Rinda announced.

She lowered herself over the battlements, hung by her hands for a moment then splashed into the moat. She trod water for a little while, waiting to see if a crocodile or a moat monster had moved in. But the moat was calm, clear, cool and empty. Not even a duck floated on its mirror-like surface.

Rinda sighed and swam ashore. She would have to find her adventure somewhere else. Fortunately, the sun was shining so she would not be a soaking wet adventurer for long.

After drying out on the grassy verge, Rinda wandered down the road, squinting at the sheep in case they were particularly cleverly disguised monsters. Then she checked under the bridge again, because a troll might have moved in since she'd last looked, yesterday afternoon. But there was no troll, only the slow flow of the river.

"Boring, boring, boring!" said Rinda. She crossed the bridge and kept going. She passed the farmhouses and more sheep. A shepherd waved at her. Rinda scowled, because until he'd waved and smiled she'd thought he might be an ogre in disguise.

Rinda kept walking and walking and walking. She walked for so long and went so far that the castle and the farmhouses disappeared out of sight behind her. Fields gave way to forest and trees closed in on the road. The sun began to sink behind the distant hills and the sky shifted colour from a cool blue to a warm and rosy red. Night was falling. Soon it would be dark.

Chapter Four

"This is more like it," said Rinda bravely, though she had to admit that she preferred daytime adventures to night-time ones. It was much easier to deal with monsters when you could see them clearly.

To be completely prepared for the adventure, Rinda picked up a fallen branch. It was almost as long as she was tall and made a hefty club. Then she turned around and started for home because it was getting very dark. Rinda knew she would be in big trouble when she got home and there was just as much chance of having an adventure on the way back.

The sun slipped away very quickly as the little girl walked along the road. *It must be tired and unable to hold itself up*, Rinda thought. She was a bit tired herself, and hungry as well. It was very unfair that she'd had to go so far and get so tired and hungry and she still hadn't had an adventure!

Rinda was almost back to the last farmhouse when the sun finally disappeared. Day became night, a night without a moon. There were some stars scattered across the sky, but they shed little light. Rinda could hardly see the road and had to tap the cobblestones with her stick so she didn't lose her way.

To make matters worse, someone had left a cart or wagon piled high with hay parked across the road. It was hard to tell in the dark, but she couldn't think of anything else about thirty feet high and fifteen feet long that might be on the road. It made her mad that someone had just left it there, blocking her way home. So she went right up to the cart and hit it with her stick.

Whack! Whack! Whack!

That's what it should have sounded like. A stick hitting wood. But it didn't. It sounded completely different.

Whomp! Whomp! Whomp!

That was the sound of a stick hitting something like leather, and carts weren't made of leather. So it wasn't a cart…

Before Rinda could do anything, whatever it was suddenly moved!

"Uh-oh," said Rinda.

The thing that blocked the road reared up until it was at least forty-five feet high, far too high to be a cartload of hay. It spread its two huge furry paws wide and its great long claws caught the starlight and shone blue and silver.

It opened its great big mouth and its sharp white teeth gleamed in the darkness.

"Mum!" screamed Rinda. "Dad!"

She hit the monster with her stick, but the stick broke on the monster's side. Then a paw closed round her and Rinda went up and up and up, and the huge mouth opened wider and wider and wider. Rinda looked down at the gleaming teeth, the big red tongue and the pulsating tonsils at the back of the monster's throat.

Rinda pushed and kicked and bit, but the monster's mouth gaped even wider, releasing a strange oily stench from deep inside.

Rinda wasn't put off. She knew what to do. "One leap!" she said to herself as she kicked her way free and dived straight past the monster's teeth and into its gullet!

Chapter Five

Rinda slid like a dollop of ice cream down the monster's tongue. She flew over its tonsils, did a corkscrew turn through its cavernous throat, then continued straight down the long, slightly icky slippery dip that was its gullet.

She opened her penknife – the one she wasn't supposed to have – on the long slide down, ready to cut her way free. Rinda knew it would take a long time, since the knife was very small and very blunt and wasn't even any good for cutting goose feathers into quill pens.

This might be a problem, Rinda thought. Her mother had told her often that a monster's stomach was a very unpleasant place to be. Full of stinks and smells and acids that could dissolve you in a few hours, just like a human stomach dissolved food. She would have to try very hard to get out as soon as possible.

But when she slid out of the end of the gullet, the monster's stomach was nothing like any stomach she'd ever heard about. In fact, it looked exactly like a very nice kitchen, the kind that her mother would have liked to have at the castle, but didn't.

The floor of this kitchen was lined with polished flagstones. There was a lovely old kitchen table with a checked blue and white tablecloth and a basket of fruit on top of it. A two-oven stove fired by magic stones sat in one corner. A hollow miniature iceberg stuck up out of the floor, magically preserving a whole lot of yummy-looking food. Crystal-fronted cupboards around the walls showed tins and boxes of food, shining silver cooking utensils, and gleaming brass pots and pans.

"Odd," said Rinda. "Suspicious even." Her mother

had never mentioned finding a kitchen inside any of the monsters that had tried to eat her alive.

Rinda folded her penknife and looked around. Apart from the opening high above, there didn't seem to be any way in or out of this strange stomach-kitchen. But there had to be.

She opened the cupboards till she found the flour. She took a handful and threw it against the walls wherever

there wasn't a cupboard. It took her only a minute to find two invisible doors and an invisible rubbish chute.

Rinda opened the first flour-coated door and looked inside. A white spiral staircase led both up and down. The steps were thin and kind of bony-looking. Rinda quickly realised that she was looking at the monster's backbone.

Only it wasn't really a monster. That was clear too now. Besides the kitchen, strange enough in itself, all around the stairs there were clear tubes full of swirling coloured fluids and she saw metal wires going up and down and little cogs turning, and everywhere there was a faint whirr and zing that Rinda recognised.

Clockwork!

She was inside a giant magical clockwork monster!

Chapter Six

Rinda looked up and down the backbone stairs. Should she go up or down?

Up, Rinda decided. Somebody must be in charge of this monster, and where else would they be but inside the creature's head? Rinda would sneak up on whoever it was and teach them a lesson. Nobody was allowed to use a giant clockwork monster to eat up a princess!

Rinda ran up the steps three at a time till the stairs suddenly ended and she hit her head on trapdoor. This hurt, but it only made Rinda even angrier. She punched the door, which immediately flipped open so she didn't even graze her knuckles.

Rinda took a peek through the trapdoor. It led to a room inside the creature's head. It was fairly dark inside, but she could see big windows where its eyes would be on the outside, and between the eyes at the back of the creature's nose there were a lot of levers and faintly glowing dials and a whole row of foot pedals. Clearly these were the controls, like the ones in her father's magical model steam engine that he wouldn't let her play with.

But no one was driving the monster. Rinda could feel a swaying motion, like being on a boat, and she could see stars going past through the eyes, so she knew they were moving.

She crept up through the trap door and on to the floor. Then she slithered over to the controls. One big lever was pulled all the way back, almost to the floor. It had a cardboard tag tied to the end. Rinda turned the tag so it picked up the light from the dials and read: *Follow the road*.

There was another smaller lever pulled down as well. It also had a tag. Rinda read that too. It said: *Don't hurt anyone*.

Just then, she heard a horrible grunting sound behind her. Forgetting to slither, she jumped up, ready to fight for her life.

There was no one there. Then the grunting sound started again, from somewhere above Rinda's head. She looked up and saw a hammock stretched right across the top of the room. Two bare feet were poking out of one end. Horrible-looking green and yellow feet that were covered in lumps and hairs.

A troll, thought Rinda. *A witch-troll*. She knew the troll was female because there was a daisy growing out of her big toe. A ghastly snoring witch-troll driving a magical clockwork monster to attack the kingdom.

But why did she have the lever pulled back that said *Don't hurt anyone?*

Rinda thought for a moment and came to the conclusion that the witch-troll wanted to take everyone alive. Maybe she ate people raw and fresh. Or maybe she wanted slaves.

Whatever the reason, Rinda knew she had to defeat the troll and break the clockwork monster. But how could she? Trolls were sword- and arrow-proof, let alone blunt-penknife-proof.

The horrible grunting sound came again, followed by an even more horrible wuffling noise. It was even more horrible because it sounded like the troll was waking up.

Rinda thought very quickly. Maybe she could entangle the troll in her own hammock… She opened her penknife, ran to the rope that held up the hammock and started sawing away. The rope twanged as Rinda cut through the first small thread.

"Who's there?" asked a voice above her. It didn't sound like a troll's voice, but Rinda didn't respond. She knew a witch-troll could imitate a human.

"Something something lumious," said the witch-troll. Rinda knew it was a spell, because it was in the magical language her father used. A second later, the room was as bright as day.

Rinda didn't look up. She just sawed even harder. She was through half a dozen threads, but there were plenty more and her penknife was very blunt.

"Something something frosty-osty," said the witch-troll. Rinda stopped sawing. She couldn't move her arms or legs or turn her head. But she could roll her eyes and she was still breathing.

She heard a thump as the witch-troll jumped down and landed behind her.

"Well, well, what have we here?" said the witch-troll. She sounded quite friendly, but Rinda knew that was a trick. "Come to join me for dinner?"

"Come and be dinner," was what Rinda heard.

There was only one thing to do. Rinda took a very, very deep breath and let out the special scream her parents had taught her. A screaming spell that her father had made, that Rinda's mother and father would always hear no matter where she was. A scream that she knew could only be used in matters of life and death.

"Heeeeeeeeeeeeeeeeeeeeeeeeeeeeeeeeeeeelp!"

Things happened surprisingly quickly then. The witch-troll said something and Rinda fell to the floor, but only because she hadn't expected her legs to unfreeze. She landed on her hands and immediately did a backflip – a standard warrior maiden move – and tried to kick the witch-troll in the head, even though she knew it wouldn't do any good.

But instead of bouncing off iron-hard troll flesh, Rinda felt herself caught by soft hands, just like when her mother was teaching her backflips. The surprise made her pause for a fateful second. At least it would have been fateful if the witch-troll really had been a witch-troll. But she wasn't. She was a nice-looking old lady who was wearing a purple night-dress and troll-foot slippers.

"You must be Princess Chlorinda," said the nice old lady. "I'm—"

Whatever she was going to say was lost as the clockwork monster suddenly lurched to one side. The old lady dropped the princess and they both fell over.

Before they could get up there was a tremendous booming sound from somewhere below. A shower of arrows clattered like hail across the eye-windows of the monster, followed a second later by jagged streaks of lightning that jumped all over the place. There was shouting and screaming and oinking and banging and clanging and small explosions.

The clockwork monster shuddered under these attacks, stumbled and fell on its knees. Rinda and the old woman were thrown against the levers. As she tried to stop herself, Rinda accidentally pulled up the small lever that was marked *Don't hurt anyone.*

Bells rang inside the monster's head. An ominous red light flashed out from its eyes and it raised its mighty claws.

Chapter Seven

"No!" cried the old woman. She lunged forward and pushed the lever back down, then quickly pulled another one and pushed a button. The clockwork monster gave out a long, mechanical hiss and its head sagged forward till its nose touched the ground. The old woman touched another button and the top of the monster's head lifted open like a big hatch.

They had stopped right outside the castle and a large crowd had gathered in a semicircle around the monster.

"Surrender!" ordered King Victor sternly, a jar of

jumping-spark ointment in one hand and a teaspoon for throwing it in the other.

"Release my daughter!" added Queen Alba, her two-handed sword held high above her head, ready for action.

"Don't move!" shouted the guard, who had an arrow nocked on his longbow.

"Or we'll hook you!" shouted the shepherds, making menacing moves with their crooks.

"And stick you," yelled the farmers, shaking their pitchforks.

"Oink!" added Horace the pig.

Rinda ran out of the monster's head. The jumping-spark ointment and two-handed sword were thrown aside as the king and queen embraced their daughter.

"I did it!" said Rinda. "I leaped past its teeth in one go and went straight down its gullet. Only it wasn't a normal monster, it's a clockwork monster, and there's a witch-troll inside, only she's not a witch-troll, she's a… I don't know what she is…"

"Mmmm," said King Victor as he looked past Rinda at the old woman who was gingerly climbing out of the monster's head.

"Uh-oh," said Queen Alba as the old woman marched towards them.

"Got to go and polish a helmet," mumbled the guard as he tried to hide his longbow behind a small tree.

"That the sheep calling?" muttered the shepherds as they milled about, while trying to get further away without turning their backs.

"Bedtime already," the farmers confirmed to each other as they hastily stepped off into the darkness

"Uh-hoinch," muttered Horace.

"You've broken my clockwork monster," said the old woman.

"Sorry, Aunt Daisy," said Queen Alba very quietly.

"Our apologies, Aunt-in-Law," said the king in his most formal voice.

"Uh-oh," said Rinda.

"As I was saying, before we were so rudely interrupted," the old woman said to Rinda, "you must be Princess Chlorinda. I am your Great Aunt Daisy, Consulting Witch-Engineer. I have come to visit for the school holidays."

"I'm sorry I broke your clockwork monster," said Rinda. "I just wanted to have an adventure."

"Perfectly understandable," said Great Aunt Daisy. "Your mother was just the same, though I don't believe she managed to get past the teeth of a monster and go straight down the gullet until she was at least ten."

"Ten and a half," said Queen Alba. She smiled at her daughter. "And it was only a monstrous slug beetle, not a giant clockwork mechanical monster."

"And you managed to find the secret doors in the stomach," said Great Aunt Daisy. "I am impressed."

Rinda looked at her father, who glanced down at her flour-stained hands. He winked and smiled. Rinda smiled back. She wasn't going to reveal his secret.

"Now," said Great Aunt Daisy, "I think we should all go and have dinner. Rinda and I can come back in the morning to fix my monster. If you don't have anything better to do, that is, my dear."

Rinda looked across at the monster. She'd only seen a little bit of its insides, and not much of its outsides at all, in the dark. There would be all manner of interesting corners and mechanisms and tunnels and secrets in the clockwork monster.

"I don't exactly have anything better to do," she said. "But there is one thing that I need to take care of first."

"What?" asked Queen Alba and King Victor.

Rinda stared at them. Had they forgotten already? She pointed at her pet pig.

"There's a beastly beast on the... well, it *was* on the battlements, now it's... lurking in the darkness. A bloody... well, it *was* bloody... now it's a muddy beastly beast and we have to sort it out!"

"Of course," said Great Aunt Daisy. She strode over the road, grabbed Horace by the ear and pointed him towards the castle. "We'll wash him in the moat on the way in. Anything else?"

Everyone looked at Rinda. She opened her mouth, took a deep breath, held it for a few seconds, then slowly shook her head. So they all went happily into the castle for dinner.

Bill the Inventor

Chapter One

When Bill was a very small baby, he was found on the street, wrapped in a really big banana skin.

The man who found him was hungry. So he was very disappointed to find a squirmy baby inside the banana skin instead of a tasty piece of fruit.

The man tried to find Bill's parents.

He went to the supermarket to see if anyone had bought a really big banana recently. He tried the hospital to see if anyone was missing a baby boy.

He put an ad in the newspaper, which unfortunately

got mixed up so it said, "Found: small banana inside baby boy".

But he couldn't find Bill's parents.

So he decided he'd better put him in an orphanage, which is a home for children whose parents have died or disappeared.

So Bill was sent to the O'Squealin Home for Lost Children. It was called the O'Squealin Home because that was the name of the lady who managed it – Mrs O'Squealin.

Why it was called the Home for Lost Children no one knew. The children weren't lost. It was their parents who were mislaid.

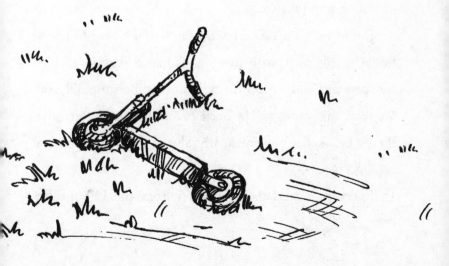

Chapter Two

Bill was very happy at the O'Squealin Home. Mrs O'Squealin was basically good at heart and there were lots of children to play with.

But as he grew older, he did think that he might like a home of his own, with two well-behaved parents to buy him presents and pay for his experiments. Because Bill, you see, was an inventor. He liked to invent things, and the things he liked to invent nearly always needed expensive bits and pieces.

Every now and then, children from the O'Squealin

Home did get new parents. This was called adoption. If you were lucky enough to get picked, then you would be adopted.

Sometimes the new parents weren't good enough for the children, so there was a special thirty-day guarantee. If not completely satisfied, the child could come back to the O'Squealin Home and wait for some better parents to come along.

Chapter Three

One day, when Bill was inventing a new way of spooning cornflakes into his mouth using six rubber bands, a spoon and four of the attic mice in a treadwheel, Mrs O'Squealin came in and said, "Finish up quickly, Bill. There are some parents here to have a look at you."

Bill had never been picked for adoption before. He was so excited he drank his bowl of cornflakes in one gulp and ran down to the special room where new parents waited.

A strange sound inside the room – like a squawking

parrot – made Bill stop and look through the glass panel in the door.

The room was full of people, far too many for just one set of parents. They looked pretty strange too, with their coats of red and black, and their wide leather belts holding cutlasses and pistols. One even had an eyepatch, and he saw a pegleg and a parrot.

"Pirates!" Bill whispered. They must have done away with the parents who had come to adopt him!

Quickly, Bill turned to run to the phone to call the police. But before he could move, a strong bony hand gripped him by the shoulder. For a second he thought a pirate had him, but then Mrs O'Squealin spoke.

"You were quick, Bill," she said. "Now come along and meet Captain and Mrs Blood and their charming crew."

"What!" exclaimed Bill, unable to believe his ears. "You can't mean they're the parents who I'm supposed to go with? They're PIRATES!"

"Stop yelling, Bill," said Mrs O'Squealin calmly, as she opened up the door and pushed him in. "You don't want the Bloods to get the wrong idea and think you're a naughty boy."

They would probably be pleased, thought Bill. How could Mrs O'Squealin possibly give him to pirates? She must have been bribed with gold doubloons or a piece of sunken silver treasure.

Inside the room, the pirates looked at Bill. He stared back suspiciously, wondering what on earth they wanted with a boy. They probably needed him for some terrible scheme. Perhaps a tunnel, dark and secret, through which only a boy could crawl – to get inside a fortress and open up the gate. Or to be a spy in some merchant's ship, signalling to the pirates with a lantern when the night was dark and starless.

All exciting stuff, no doubt, if you happened to have a pirate heart. But Bill was an inventor and there are things an inventor just doesn't do.

"Here's the boy," said Mrs O'Squealin to Captain Blood, the biggest, meanest, nastiest looking pirate of them all. "He goes by the name of Bill."

Captain Blood had a red beard divided into seven sections, each one bound tightly with a bright red rubber band. Every now and again he'd flick one of the bands and scream as it snapped him in the face.

Bill thought that was a very stupid thing to do, but then pirates weren't known for being smart.

"Ah-har," said Captain Blood, smiling to show that his teeth had been filed to extremely nasty points. "Look here, Mrs Blood. It's our new son!"

Mrs Blood was even taller and meaner looking than the captain. She wore a grimy leather dress hung with long chains of tiny shrunken heads that even Bill could see were fake and made of rubber. Her eyes kept crossing and she hissed with every second word.

"Come here-ss, my boy-ss," she said, reaching out to hug Bill in her rubbery-skulled embrace. But he ducked in

under her arms and tried to squeeze himself through the window, only to be caught by Mrs O'Squealin, with one strong hand around his ankle.

"I'm an inventor!" shouted Bill. "Not a pirate. I'll never go with them."

"What!" roared Captain Blood. "What kind of boy are you? We sail at dawn to cross the seven seas in our ship the *Salty Sally*. A hundred adventures lie in wait, including tons of buried treasure. There's cutlass fights and cannons roaring and the wind fierce-blowing in our sails. Why, when I was a lad I'd have sold my own parents to have the chance of joining up with pirates!"

"I heard you did," said Mrs O'Squealin, dragging Bill back in and sitting him on a chair. "But we do have rules here at the O'Squealin Home. If Bill doesn't want you for his mum and dad, then he doesn't have to go. And if he does go, he still has thirty days to change his mind."

"Is that so?" the captain roared.

His hand went to his cutlass, but Mrs Blood whispered something in his ear. No one else was meant to hear, but Bill did, for his ears were very sharp.

"In thirty-ss days-ss," he heard her say, "we'll-ss be at-ss sea and then-ss he'll have-ss no choice-ss."

"No way," said Bill. "It's like I said. I'm an inventor, not a pirate."

"Well we just might take you anyway," sneered Captain Blood, drawing out his cutlass.

But Bill was even quicker on the draw and his pockets were full of inventions. He pulled out something that looked like a cross between a small electric drill and a set of artificial teeth.

"This is the fang-o-rotor," said Bill in a very serious voice. "It has never been tested on humans. Do you want to be the first?"

Captain Blood stared at the fang-o-rotor and his face began to pale. He put the cutlass back and joined the other pirates where they huddled against the wall, as far away from Bill as they could get.

"Now get out!" shouted Bill, pressing the trigger to whiz the teeth around. "Once I start it I don't know if it will stop."

"Arrrrrrrggggghhhhh!" the pirates screamed as they ran out through the door, all except for Mrs Blood, who dived out through the window screaming, "Arrrrrrrggggg hhhhh-ssss!"

As the last pirate disappeared out of the door, the gnashing teeth of the fang-o-rotor slowed to a not very scary chomp.

"Flat battery," said Bill. "Or else I made it wrong."

"Hhhhmmmmppph!" exclaimed Mrs O'Squealin, taking the fang-o-rotor and putting it up on a shelf too high for

Bill to reach. "You and your inventions! A perfectly fine set of parents scared away. You should have at least tried them for the thirty days, Bill. You might have come to like the pirate life."

"But I'm an inventor," said Bill. "Maybe I should invent my own parents."

"Don't you dare," said Mrs O'Squealin. "It's my job to find parents for you and I don't want any more inventions getting in the way. Now, it's time for lessons, so off you go."

Chapter Four

Bill thought that by scaring off the pirates he had ruined his chances of ever being picked for adoption again. But the very next day, while he was in the garden making an invention out of a coffee jar, four chopsticks, the garden hose and a spare roller skate, Mrs O'Squealin called out of the window to him.

"Bill! Bill! Stop whatever you're doing and come in. I've got some more parents for you to try."

Bill was extremely wet due to the garden hose being on

while he was experimenting with it, but he didn't stop to change. Inventors don't spare any thought for things like fresh clothes or cleaning up.

To make sure Mrs O'Squealin wasn't trying the pirates on him again, Bill peeked through the glass panel in the door.

This time, there were only two people waiting – a tall man with a long white beard, who wore a flowing robe of darkest black, covered in silver stars and golden moons. His wife looked almost exactly the same, except she had long white hair instead of a beard, and her robe had golden stars and silver moons. Both wore black pointy hats which shaded their faces so Bill couldn't see their eyes.

Bill knew instantly that they were a wizard and a witch. This seemed a bit more promising than pirates, especially as an inventor could use a little magic.

Perhaps these two would be good parents, at least worth trying for thirty days. He raised his hand to knock, but before he could, the wizard opened the door.

"Hello," he said, in a voice that seemed to come from long ago and far away. "You are Bill. I am the Wizard Walter Wenish and this is my wife, the Witch of the North-by-Northwest. You may call her Emily. We would like to adopt you."

"Hmmm," said Bill. "Can I ask a few questions, first, before I make up my mind?"

"A tower by the sea, where you can have your own room," replied Emily. "You won't have to go to school because we will teach you wizardry and witchcraft. I'm not sure about inventions."

"You read my mind," said Bill, who'd only just thought of the questions about where they lived, whether he'd have his own room, whether he'd have to go to school and, the most important of all, whether he'd be allowed to make inventions.

"I'm sure we could cope with a certain amount of invention-making," Walter added. "Say an hour per week. The rest of your time will have to be spent in serious study of course –

Algebra, Trigonometry, Astrology, Alchemy, Spellcraft, Magic, Mystery and Needlework."

"It's traditional for wizards and witches to make their own clothes," explained Emily, reading Bill's mind again. "But it won't be all work, Bill. We'll also have our midnight picnics, out on the marshes. We'll be chasing toads to roast on sticks with cave-fungus cakes, all washed down with stinging-nettle wine. You'll love it.

"Roasted toads? Fungus cakes? One hour of invention per week?" said Bill. "No way. I'm an inventor, not a wizard."

"Oh no, Bill, you can't turn down Mr and Mrs Wenish!" exclaimed Mrs O'Squealin.

"Why not?" asked Bill.

"Because we'll turn you both into toads," said Emily the Witch of the North-by-Northwest, tipping her hat back so Bill could see an evil redness glowing in her eyes.

"And then we'll roast you for our midnight picnic," added Walter, pulling his hands out of his pockets to point his long, yellow and ever-so-sharp fingernails at Bill.

"So you see, you simply can't refuse," said Mrs

O'Squealin. "Think of what would happen to all the other children if I was turned into a roasted toad!"

Bill nodded, as if he was going to go along, but his hands went to his pockets. Both of them were full of water, plus a few inventing-type odds and ends. Including lots of little magnets that Bill had picked off the orphanage fridge.

Bill knew that if there's one thing witches and wizards are afraid of, it's magnetised water.

"My pockets are full of magnetised water," Bill said in a very serious voice. "If you don't leave right away, both of you will get it."

"Don't try some silly trick on me," said Walter, but then he saw that Emily was already edging towards the door.

She'd read Bill's mind and knew that he really did have the water in his pockets. Just one drop of magnetised water could confuse a witch or wizard for a week. They wouldn't know up from down, north from south, day from night, or roasted toad from cornflakes. Bill had two whole handfuls of magnetised water in his pockets, enough to confuse twenty wizards for a year.

"Only joking," Walter muttered nervously, watching his wife slip out of the door. "Wouldn't think of turning anyone into toads, least of all you two. Shouldn't be taken seriously. Just a joke. Really, is it quite so late? Must be off. It's been a pleasure. Perhaps some other time."

When he got to the door, he opened it just a crack and practically slithered through. Bill pulled his hands out of his pockets and let them drip upon the floor.

"So that's where the fridge magnets went," said Mrs O'Squealin sternly. "Well, I suppose that this time it was for the best. I don't know about your inventions, Bill, but obviously I'll have to work harder to find suitable parents for you."

Bill nodded, but he wasn't very confident, given the first two sets of parents Mrs O'Squealin had shown him.

Chapter Five

Mrs O'Squealin didn't stop trying to find new parents for Bill. Only the next day she tracked him down up in the attic, where he was trying to convince some mice to try out a fleet of rubber-band-powered biplanes built to his own design. But the mice had worked with Bill's inventions in the past and didn't want to fly. Bill was hoping a piece of cheese would change their minds.

"Leave those mice alone and come downstairs,"

commanded Mrs O'Squealin. "Some more parents want to check you out."

"Don't try the biplanes without me," said Bill to the mice. He didn't realise that saying this would make them try for sure. Mice hate being told what to do.

"Now, Bill, these particular parents look a bit... well... odd," said Mrs O'Squealin as they went down the stairs. "But they seem very nice and... interesting."

Bill wasn't listening. He was thinking about inventing some special steps that you could lie on so that they massaged your back on the way down.

He was so busy thinking about how you would get back up these special steps that he walked into the parent room without looking through the window.

"This is Bill," said Mrs O'Squealin – from out in the

corridor. Then she slammed the door and made a sound like she was going to throw up.

Bill felt like he was going to be sick too. Mrs O'Squealin had really done it this time. She'd locked him in a room with two hideously squidgy, lumpy, slimy, sweaty, yellow-tentacled, bulbous-eyed ALIENS!

"Hello, Earth-boy Bill," one of them said. Its voice came out of a small black box it wore around what might possibly be its neck, where all the tentacles bunched together into a ghastly lump that had poppy eyes all over it. "I am Mr Smith. This is Mrs Smith, my blob wife. You can call us Mum and Dad."

Bill backed up as far as the door and reached into his pockets, feeling desperately for some invention he didn't know he had.

"Why do you want me?" he asked, trying to speak without breathing through his nose. The aliens smelled really bad, like the stuff Mrs O'Squealin used to clean the toilet, only stronger.

"This is where we get our kids," said Mrs Smith, waving several tentacles around. "We don't have children ourselves. We just pick them up on Earth and take them back to Planet Squidgeron to turn them into us."

"You mean that you were once a human girl?" asked Bill, hoping he'd heard her wrong. So far he hadn't found an invention he could use.

"Of course," said Mrs Smith. "I was picked up when I was five. And Mr Smith was too. Then we went to Squidgeron and got put in the machine. You go in human, all ugly and strange, and come out the other end as beautiful as me. You can even choose how many tentacles you want and the colour of your eyes."

"I like the way I am," said Bill, "though I see how the tentacles could be handy. So I think I'll stay here at the Home, thank you all the same."

"Our spaceship's parked right outside," said Mr Smith. With a lightning flick, he wrapped one fat tentacle around Bill's arms and slowly drew him close. "You'll like the trip

to Squidgeron. We have some DVDs for you to watch along the way. Educational DVDs that explain why tentacles are great, and the benefits of having thirty-three eyes instead of two.

"I won't go!" shouted Bill. "No way! I'm an inventor, not a Squidgeron!"

But in his heart he knew he didn't have a hope. Mr

Smith's tentacle had trapped his arms down at his sides and he couldn't get at his pockets. Even if he had an invention there, he couldn't reach it.

This time it looked like he'd have to go along. To planet Squidgeron, to get turned into a blobby thing that smelled disgusting and made humans throw up their lunch.

"Just this way," said Mr Smith, dragging Bill out through the door. There was no sign of Mrs O'Squealin or any other kids. Bill didn't blame them. If he'd seen the aliens first, he'd have run away in a flash.

When they were outside, Bill tried to kick himself free, but Mr Smith just wrapped another tentacle around his legs and held him up above the ground. The tentacles didn't look like much, but they were really strong, stronger even than Mrs O'Squealin's legendary grip of steel.

The spaceship was parked on the lawn. A gleaming silver saucer, it rested on three springy legs. The door was open, with a ramp leading down.

Bill stared at the ship and knew that he had only a minute more of freedom. Once he was in the ship it would be too late for any tricks.

Chapter Six

Desperately Bill looked around, hoping to see something he could use or somebody to help. And then he heard it, high above – the drone of rubber-band engines starting up. Tilting his head back as far as the tentacle would let him, Bill saw that the mice were preparing to launch the biplanes from the roof. All twenty aircraft he'd made with care, each one piloted by a brave and clever mouse.

"Help!" cried Bill. "I'm being kidnapped! Please attack at once."

Up on the roof, the mouse squadron leader looked down and narrowed his pink eyes. "Aliens at twelve o'clock," he squeaked. He didn't know what it meant but it seemed to be the right thing to say even if it was only ten in the morning.

"We'll attack out of the sun!"

Instantly, extra mice ran to the planes to sit behind the pilots, their anti-cat crossbows at the ready. Rubber bands wound to their tightest, they waited for the word to go.

This took a little longer than it should as the squadron leader had to explain what attacking out of the sun meant. They would dive down with the sun behind them so it shone in the aliens' eyes. This was bad for humans but should be even worse for the Squidgerons, he explained, because they had so many eyes to get blinded.

"Hurry up!" shouted Bill as the first biplane wheeled down the roof and shot into the air. Mr Smith was walking fast – on his tentacles instead of legs. In another second they'd be up the ramp and it would be too late.

Bill shut his eyes and held his breath. Perhaps it might be the last breath he ever had of good, clean Earth-person air. He'd never see the Home again through two normal earthling eyes, or walk across the lawn on feet instead of slimy tentacles.

Then the black box around Mr Smith's neck suddenly went. "Ouch! Ow! Heavens, I've been shot!"

Bill felt the tentacles around him slacken.

With one desperate surge of energy, he managed to break free! He hit the ground hard and it hurt a lot, but he forced himself to roll away. Bill knew the aliens' tentacles were long.

But Mr and Mrs Smith had no time to think of Bill. They rushed up the ramp, their tentacles waving in the air, trying to shield themselves from a constant rain of crossbow bolts.

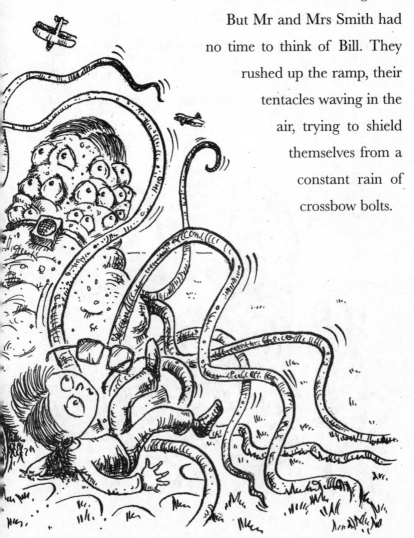

"I hate this planet!" screamed Mrs Smith as she closed the spaceship door. "We're never coming here again. We'll go to Pluto and get an ice boy there instead!"

Bill lay on his back, absolutely still, and watched the spaceship soundlessly fly straight up into the sky. The mice flew after it for a while, but as the rubber bands began to lose their twist, they circled back and landed on the lawn. Hurrying from their cockpits, they gathered around Bill, thinking he was dead.

"He was a great inventor," said the squadron leader mouse, taking off his helmet and holding it across his white furred chest. "A boy who could have gone far. He will be missed."

"I'm not dead," said Bill, without getting up. "It's just that being kidnapped by aliens is a bit of a shock. Not to mention having to deal with evil wizards and witches – and pirates who can't take no for an answer."

The squadron leader nodded in understanding, saluted and marched away to help the others rewind the rubber bands. He knew Bill needed some time alone – thinking time. Bill had to come up with a new invention that could help him forget the troubles of the day.

Chapter Seven

Bill lay there for a long time, staring at the blue sky, feeling the lawn being comfortable and sort of annoying and ticklish at the same time. But try as he might, he couldn't think of any new inventions that he could get up and make.

He was still trying to think when he fell asleep. While he slept, the mice flew away, back up to their attic. But they left four crossbow mice behind to guard him, in case the aliens came back.

Bill woke to hear one of these mice squeaking, quite close to his ear.

"Halt! Who goes there? Advance one and be recognised!"

"Um," replied a voice he didn't know. A grown-up woman's voice. "Does that mean I advance one step or that one of us should advance? And since we haven't met, I don't see how you can recognise us, do you?"

"That's just what it says in the book," squeaked the mouse, clearly embarrassed. "And there's supposed to be a password too."

"Would any password do?" asked another voice, a grown-up man's voice.

The combination of the two instantly sparked an alarm in Bill's head. A man and a woman. Obviously they were more parents come to adopt him!

"Perhaps I could invent a password?" asked the woman.

"How does humbuzzle sound?"

"Humbuzzle," repeated the mouse. "Pass friend!"

Bill opened one eye to look suspiciously at the man and woman who were standing above him.

They looked reasonable enough, almost like normal human beings. Both were wearing sensible overalls, and they had pockets stuffed full of odds and ends.

The man was wearing a hat that was clearly of his own invention, because it had a solar panel for collecting electricity on the top. And the woman had a handbag on wheels that followed after her like a dog.

"Excuse me," said the woman, "we're looking for a baby boy that was probably handed in. We had a mix-up when our automatic baby-minding and -feeding robot wrapped the baby in a banana skin and the banana in a blanket. By the time we found out, we were halfway to Jupiter and it took a while for us to invent our way back. We did send lots of message rockets, but they kept blowing up."

"When was this?" asked Bill, getting to his feet.

"Mmmm?" replied the woman, who was distracted by a flight of mouse-piloted biplanes passing overhead.

"When?" demanded Bill. "When did you lose your baby?"

"Space travel does funny things to your sense of time," replied the woman. "But it was certainly far too long ago. We've missed him dreadfully. Let me check."

She pulled a diary out of her bag and started looking through it. The man reached into his pocket and pulled out a complex electronic device with a panel of lights and buttons.

"Oh dear, it's been even longer than we thought," said the man. "My computi-mem-ometer says it was more than eight years ago!"

"So does my diary," exclaimed the woman in surprise. "This is terrible! We got back as fast as we could! Now we'll have to invent a special machine to track him down."

"No you won't," said Bill, who knew just who these people had to be. They were obviously inventors and his long-lost parents!

"You mean…" said the parents, both at the same time, "you're our long-lost boy and we're your mum and dad?"

"Yep. I'm Bill the Inventor," said Bill. "But *you* got lost, not me. I was always here. Now, before we go I want to get one thing straight. I like to invent every day between the hours of ten and three, and sometimes in the middle of the night. Is that going to be OK?"

"Only between the hours of ten and three?" asked Dad. "Take all the time you want."

"We'll have to extend the laboratory," said Mum. "There's not room enough for three. Perhaps you'd like to draw a plan and we can go shopping for some things?"

"OK," said Bill. "But first you have to talk to Mrs O'Squealin and sign an awful lot of papers."

"It's not as easy as that," protested Mrs O'Squealin, who'd seen Bill's parents arrive and had come out to see what was going on. "We can't let just anyone adopt our children here. There are procedures to follow and forms to fill out, and then the thirty day trial."

"That's for people who've come to adopt," said Bill. "These are my real parents. They're inventors and they've come to take me home."

"Not without the proper forms," said Mrs O'Squealin, who really did care about the children she looked after even if she didn't understand that an inventor simply couldn't become a pirate, a wizard or an alien.

"We do have his birth certificate," said Bill's mother, pulling a large and official-looking document out of her wheely bag. It had several fancy stamps on it and two smudgy footprints, made when Bill was born.

"That could be anyone's birth certificate," declared Mrs O'Squealin.

"Take off your shoes, Bill," said Bill's dad, pulling out a fancy device with an eyehole at one end and something like a camera on the other. "My compa-pola-rometer will show this lady that your footprints match the ones on your birth certificate. They're like fingerprints. Everyone has a different pattern."

Bill sat down and quickly pulled off his shoes. His dad pointed the compa-pola-rometer at his feet and then at the footprints on the form. The machine hummed away for a moment, then a green light came on and it played a little tune, while a tinny voice inside said,

"It's a perfect match!"

"Well, I guess you must be Bill's parents," agreed Mrs O'Squealin, looking at the compa-pola-rometer and then at the man and woman who were so obviously inventors. "Now I look at you I see there is a family resemblance. But you left Bill alone for eight years! He might want to stay here."

"No way," said Bill, taking his mum and dad by the hand. "I'm an inventor, not an orphan."

Serena
and the
Sea Serpent

Chapter One

Serena Smith was the youngest of the seventeen children of Sam and Susan Smith. She had sixteen older sisters, which made people feel sorry for her. But only the people who didn't know her.

The people who knew Serena were sorry for the sisters, because Serena was the smartest, most know-it-all girl in the Smith family. She was the smartest girl in the town of Blubber Point. She was possibly the smartest girl in the whole of Australia or even the world.

Serena didn't mean to be such a terrible know-it-all. It was just that when she was a very small baby, her father used to take her into his secret laboratory, where he was inventing the most advanced computer of all time: the SuperMind.

One day, while baby Serena was

playing with the computer's mouse, lightning struck the laboratory. At the same moment, the SuperMind finished thinking about the contents of fifty-seven encyclopaedias in twelve different languages.

After the lightning hit, there was nothing left of the SuperMind computer, but everything it had been thinking about had somehow transferred into Serena's brain. Since the SuperMind had taught Serena everything, her parents and sisters spent the next seven years trying to teach her to keep all this knowledge to herself.

They tried and tried to explain to Serena that people didn't always like being told how to do things better. Sometimes people liked to work out things for themselves.

By the time Serena was eight, she knew when not to tell people how to do things. Most of the time.

So she kept her mighty brain tuned by telling her sisters what to do and stayed out of strangers' business. Most of the time.

But every now and then something came up that was so interesting that Serena had to interfere. Like the time when a sea serpent started wrecking ships from Blubber Point. So many boats and ships were damaged, always at night, that the mayor called a meeting.

Serena went along to see what she could do.

Chapter Two

The town meeting was held on the beach, with everyone sitting on deck chairs, looking out to sea. The mayor stood with her trousers rolled up, on the edge of the surf.

At first there was a lot of talk, about guns and torpedoes and harpoons and strange serpent-hunters who had eyes of different colours and spent hours carving shapes out of whalebone. Shouting above the surf, the mayor told them all to be quiet.

"That's all been tried in other parts," declared the mayor. "And it didn't work. We must give the sea serpent a child.

They've done it at Seaview, Port Picky, Mermouth and Jinn. All the towns have done it, because it's the only thing that sends the serpent on its way. Somebody will have to give up one of their children. Hands up if you've got one spare."

No one put their hand up. They didn't want to give up one of their children! The sea serpent would eat it, for sure. At least, none of the other children had ever been seen again in Seaview, Port Picky, Mermouth or Jinn.

Then Serena climbed up on the shoulders of a man who was asleep in his chair and called out, "I'll go and see this sea serpent. I bet no one's tried just talking to it. Maybe I can sort something out."

"Serena Smith, I believe," said the mayor, smiling so much that the two gold teeth at the sides of her mouth shone in the sun. Last year, Serena had told the mayor how to do her job better. "We accept."

Chapter Three

So Serena Smith was put in a rowing boat, and the mayor and two muscly rowers took her out to a small rock in the middle of the sea. They put Serena on the rock and handed over a torch and a ham sandwich wrapped in plastic.

"When night falls, shine the torch out to sea," said the mayor. "That will attract the sea serpent. The sandwich is for you, in case the serpent's late."

Then she laughed nastily and they rowed away, leaving Serena all alone on the tiny rock, where every seventh wave washed across her feet. Serena wasn't bothered by that. She could swim five kilometres backstroke and read a book at the same time. Besides, she knew the tide was falling.

Soon the sea was much lower and the sun was setting in the west, casting a red light across the water. Serena turned on her torch and shone it into the night. By her calculations, the sea serpent would be there within the hour. It always sank ships shortly after sunset.

Sure enough, the sun had hardly set before Serena saw two enormous eyes coming through the dark of the sea, coming straight for her. Behind the eyes she could see a huge bendy body of shiny scales and she knew it must be the sea serpent!

A second later, the sea serpent ran into the rock with a terrible crash and a horrible howl that nearly deafened Serena. If she'd been on a ship it would have sunk instantly, but the rock was stronger than the serpent.

The huge monster backed off and then ran into the rock again, its enormous eyes glowing in the light of Serena's torch.

Chapter Four

Serena's mighty brain worked quickly. Seeing the serpent thrash about blindly, she quickly turned off her torch and called out into the darkness.

"Sorry, Mr or Mrs Serpent! I didn't mean to scare you!"

The serpent eyed her suspiciously. Even with the light turned off, the moonlight showed Serena that the monster was as long as ten buses and it had a mouth the size of a dustcart's cruncher. It didn't seem at all happy to see Serena on the rock.

"They haven't left you for me, have they?" it boomed.

"Yes," said Serena. "I think you're supposed to eat me and stop terrorising all the boats from Blubber Point."

"Yuck!" spat the serpent. "I'm a vegetarian. I wish you people would stop giving me little girls to eat. And I wish you'd stop putting such bright lights all over the place. They blind me and I get a headache. I'm a night creature, you know."

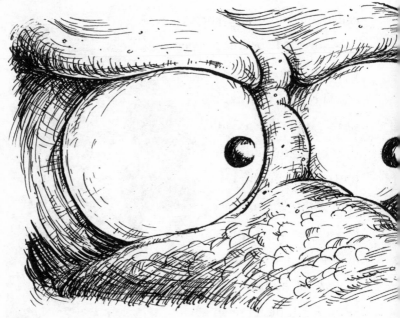

"Does that mean you're not going to eat me?" asked Serena.

"Definitely not," said the serpent. "I suppose I'll have

to take you back to Serpent Island and put you with the others."

"The other girls?" asked Serena, who'd been thinking very quickly. "Why not just take me back to the beach? I can sort things out for you. About the lights and the girls who keep being put on rocks for you."

"No," said the serpent grumpily. "I'm too big. I can only swim in very deep water. You'll have to come with me to Serpent Island."

"No thanks," said Serena. "I'll just swim home."

The serpent shook its huge head. "Too many sharks. You'd be eaten for sure. I'll have to take you to the island. Another mouth to feed and I've hardly got any weed harvested tonight. Here, climb aboard my head."

It laid its head down close to the rock till it was nearly all underwater with only the flat part between its stubby horns showing. Serena looked at it and wondered whether it was telling the truth about the sharks.

Then she decided that she really should go and see what had happened to the other girls, so she jumped across and landed on the serpent's head.

Chapter Five

Serpent Island was a very tall rock that stuck out of the sea like a needle. By the time Serena got there the moon was high in the night sky, so she could see quite clearly.

But there was no sign of the other girls.

"Where is everyone?" she asked. It looked a bit suspicious. Maybe the serpent was going to eat her after all.

"Probably underwater," said the sea serpent grumpily. "Eating all the weed I saved for my dinner."

"Underwater!" exclaimed Serena. "But they'll drown!"

"No they won't," said the serpent. It rested its head against the rock so Serena could scramble off, on to a narrow ledge that went all

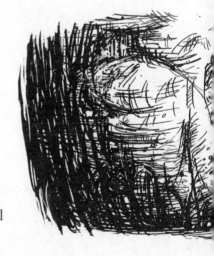

the way around the island. "I've turned them into penguimaids."

"Penguimaids?" asked Serena. She'd never heard that word before, even with all the fifty-seven encyclopaedias in her head. "What are they?"

"Girls who turn into penguins when they touch the sea," explained the serpent. "It's a spell I learned from a nixie many years ago. You see, I couldn't take the girls back so I had to do something. At least when they're penguimaids they can live out here. Though they have to eat my special seaweed or the spell wears off."

Serena nodded wisely. She knew that a nixie (also known as a nicker, nisse or nix) was a sort of water fairy.

And since the serpent couldn't return the girls, it made sense to help them live out here, at least for the time being. But it would be much better if they could be returned home. And something had to be done to stop the serpent running into ships at night.

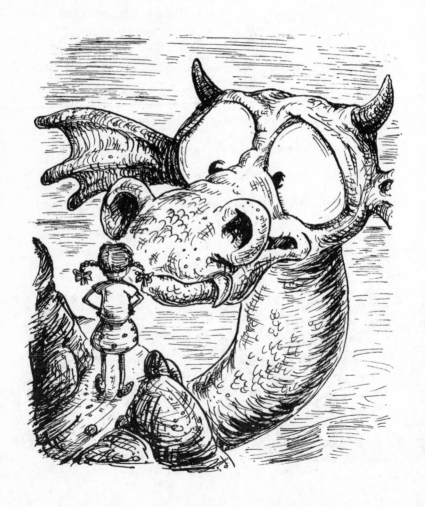

"I'll have to go even further north now," complained the serpent. "Blubber Point will just put out another girl if I go back there, and there's twenty-five of them eating me out of seaweed already. But first I need to turn you into a penguimaid."

"You did say this spell wears off if I don't eat the special seaweed?" asked Serena cautiously.

"Yes," said the serpent. "And if you get far enough from the sea, you'll turn back into a girl. Not that any of them here seem to want to change back. I think they like being penguins."

"Nonsense," said Serena. "I'm sure I'll want to change back. Now get on with the spell. I think that once I'm a penguin I might be able to help you."

Chapter Six

But once Serena was a penguimaid, she didn't want to change back.

It was so much fun zooming around after shoals of bright silver fish, sucking them into her fat black and white stomach and following them up with a nice salad of seaweed from the serpent's pantry at the bottom of the sea.

The other penguimaids were nice too, though being penguins they couldn't talk.

But they all played underwater games together, like follow-the-leader, zipping up and down and around in circles and spirals and doing backward somersaults and complicated twists.

This went on for days and days, and Serena might have stayed a penguimaid forever – until one afternoon she fell asleep on a rock in the sun and the tide went out, and she became completely dry for the first time since the serpent had cast the spell.

When she woke up, Serena wasn't a penguin any more, but a human being. She stopped thinking about fish and seaweed and swimming races, and her mighty brain sprang back into action. It was fun being a penguimaid, but it wasn't really what she wanted to do with her life.

To give herself more time in human shape, Serena climbed higher up the rock, trying to get as far away from the sea as she could. Even a little touch of spray would change her back into a penguin.

By the time the sun set, Serena was high up on the rock. But the tide was still rising, so she knew she only had a few minutes to put a plan into action.

"Sea serpent!" called out Serena. "Oh, sea serpent!"

Chapter Seven

During the day, the sea serpent slept in an underwater cave under the rocky island. But he was already awake and swimming out when he heard Serena calling, and soon his huge scaly head rose up out of the water and kept on rising and rising until it was level with Serena.

"What do you want?"
the serpent asked grumpily.
He was always grumpy
when he'd just woken up.

"I've thought of a way for you to avoid the ships at night," said Serena. "But you have to take me back as close to Blubber Point as you can, so I can swim in and organise some help for you and the girls."

"It's no good," said the serpent gloomily. "You'll turn into a penguin as soon as a drop of seawater touches you, and then you won't remember where to go or why you want to."

"Yes, I will," said Serena. "I'll hypnotise myself before I turn into a penguin."

"Hypnotise? What's that?" asked the serpent.

"It's a special way of making someone's mind do things without them thinking about them," explained Serena. "I know all about it."

"Well, I suppose it's worth a try," sighed the serpent. "I had to go five hundred kilometres last night to get enough weed for myself and you girls. All the way to Stinky Bay. And I ran into a ship, so there'll probably be another girl to collect tonight.

"It's not Stinky Bay any more," said Serena absently. She couldn't help herself being right. "They changed the name to Tropicopacabanos."

"It still stinks," said the sea serpent. "Can I watch you do this hypnotism thing?"

It only took a few minutes for Serena to hypnotise herself. She took off the charm bracelet she wore around her wrist and swung it back and forth in front of her eyes, muttering a special chant she'd learned from one of the encyclopaedias. Then she said over and over again:

Swim, Serena, swim to shore
Then go to the place you knew before
Number 77 Mullet Street
Where you'll find some fish to eat
After eating, find a nice bed
And lay down your sleepy head

After a hundred times, even the sea serpent felt like going to 77 Mullet Street. Then, just as Serena was going to repeat it for the hundred and first time, a big wave sent a plume of spray high up on to the island.

In an instant, Serena was a penguin again. She started to waddle down towards the sea, but the serpent was too quick. His huge jaws opened and a great green tongue came out and wrapped around Serena, pulling her back into the monster's mouth!

Chapter Eight

For a moment it looked like the sea serpent was going to swallow Serena whole, but he didn't. He just kept her firmly wrapped up in his tongue and started to swim towards the distant land.

The other penguimaids watched him go, but they didn't really understand what was happening. It was getting dark, and they were settling down to sleep in the little caves and hollows in the rock, just above sea level.

"Aaaaahhhhhh!" said the serpent as he rippled through the water. It was very difficult swimming with his mouth open, but it was the only way to hang on to Serena and it was a long way to Blubber Point. the serpent wasn't sure if Serena's hypnotism would work, but he wanted to get her as close to the beach as possible.

A kilometre out from Blubber Point, the serpent's belly started to hit the bottom as he swam. So he stopped and gently spat Serena into the water.

For a few seconds the penguin looked stunned, then she started to swim towards the beach and the lights beyond it that marked the town.

"Glood luckth," said the serpent. His tongue had gone to sleep from hanging on to Serena for too long. "I hopth thith workth."

Serena swam single-mindedly towards the beach. All thoughts of fish and seaweed and swimming games were gone. She just knew that she had to swim to the shore and then go somewhere.

Serena didn't see the shark that rushed at her, its many-toothed mouth open wide enough to swallow her in one gulp. But the shark was used to penguins that dodged and dived, not hypnotised penguins that swam in a straight line. It missed and, before it could stop, ran straight into the sea serpent. Dazed by the collision, the shark swam away in the opposite direction and Serena was safe.

Soon her little webbed feet were on the sand and she couldn't swim any more. So she slid on her belly and let the wash take her up as high as it could. Then she clumsily stood up and waddled across the beach, up to the car park, past the cold-water showers and the changing rooms, and across the street. Two people putting their fishing rods on their car saw her and said, "Hey, a penguin!"

But Serena waddled on. All she could think of now was a certain house, where she somehow knew that there would be fish for her and a place to sleep. She crossed another street, using the pedestrian crossing, which made a very old man who was watching call the police to report that "a black and white thingamajig just crossed at one of those black and white whatsmacallits".

Then the penguin went in the gate at 77 Mullet Street which, of course, was the Smith family home. She hopped up the steps and through the cat-door and then waddled into the dining room.

Chapter Nine

All Serena's sixteen sisters and her mum and dad were having dinner. They were very sad because they thought Serena had been eaten by the sea serpent. They ate in silence, with their heads hanging down, and no one noticed that a penguin had jumped up on to Serena's chair till the small bird tapped her beak on the table.

"Look!" said Suzy, Sally, Sapphira and Sappho.

"It's!" exclaimed Serendipity, Susan, Suky and Silvia.

"A," added Sheila, Sigrid, Sonia and Stephanie.

"PENGUIN!" shouted Stella, Sidonie, Salome and Sophie.

"Hmmm," said Mr Smith. "It looks familiar."

"It's Serena," said Mrs Smith calmly, because mothers always know their own children. "Suzy, Serendipity, go and open six or seven tins of sardines."

After eating all the sardines in the pantry and a tin of

tuna, Serena jumped down from the table and went to her old bedroom. Because their father was an inventor, he had invented special rooms for his daughters.

Suzy, Serendipity, Sheila and Stephanie each had one level of the rocket ship that their father had built in the back garden (but it had never taken off).

Sigrid and Sonia shared a very comfortable cave dug into the artificial hill their father had made for skiing on grass (but the grass hadn't grown).

Stella, Sidonie, Salome and Susan actually had small houses of their own, just big enough for a bed and a chest of drawers, all built around a fountain on the lawn. The other sisters all had rooms in the house, rooms that looked fairly normal but were special in some way.

Serena's bedroom was a secret chamber under the stairs. You couldn't even see the door to it, because it opened when you jumped up and down on the third step in a very special way.

As the penguin went to the third step, all the Smith family (except for one) held their breath. Then they all sighed with relief as the penguin stopped on the left-hand side of the step and slowly jumped up and down five times.

With a *snick*, the door under the stairs opened, revealing Serena's tidy little bedroom. The penguin yawned, jumped down between the stair rails and went into her room.

"I told you it was Serena," said her mother. She shut the door behind her penguin daughter and everyone went to bed.

Chapter Ten

When she woke up in the morning, Serena wasn't a penguin any more. She'd dried out and turned back into a girl. Because she was a bit worried she might become a penguin if she had a shower or a bath, Serena just got dressed, even though she was covered in drying salt from the sea.

Everyone was waiting for her at breakfast. In between eating cornflakes, Serena explained where she had been and how she had to do something so the sea serpent would stop running into ships and all the girls could be brought home to their families.

"What are you going to do?" shouted Suzy, Sally, Sapphira, Sappho, Serendipity, Susan, Suky, Silvia, Salome, Sheila, Sidonie, Sophie, Stella, Sigrid, Sonia and Stephanie.

Serena wouldn't tell them. For the first time in her life she wasn't sure if her plan would work. She had to talk to the mayer of Blubber Point, and then the mayors of Seaview, Port Picky, Mermouth, Jinn and Tropicopacabanos (which used to be Stinky Bay). Her plan would cost a lot of money and the towns would have to pay.

The mayor of Blubber Point was not at all pleased to see Serena.

"Does this mean the serpent will come back?" she asked as soon as Serena walked into her office. "Or does it want another girl? Someone easier to stomach?"

"The serpent is a vegetarian," Serena said. "He doesn't want anyone left out for him. And he only runs into ships because their lights blind him."

"So is it going to cause more trouble around here?" asked the mayor. She didn't care about why the serpent did what it did, only how it could be kept away from Blubber Point.

"Not if you help me with my plan," said Serena, and she smiled sweetly. "It will only cost five thousand pounds. You can write a cheque. And you'll need to help me convince the other mayors to help too."

"Five thousand pounds!" screamed the mayor. "Don't tell me you're starting to charge for being right all the time!"

"It's not for me!" said Serena. "I need it to get something for the serpent. So he won't run into ships any more."

"All right," grumbled the mayor as she wrote out a cheque. "But this had better work. What are you buying the Serpent anyway?"

Chapter Eleven

It took all day for Serena to get the money from the other mayors. Then another week before what she wanted could be made for the serpent.

In that time he had run into three more ships, all on different parts of the coast. Obviously he was having to go further and further to find the right seaweed.

Eight days after she'd first swum ashore as a penguin, Serena went out one afternoon in a large cruiser, heading for Serpent Island. Her oldest sister, Suzy (who was a sailor), steered and the other sisters helped Serena with a package that was as long as three sisters lying down head to toe and as wide as one sister was tall (or one and a quarter if it was Stella, the shortest of them all).

The mayors of Blubber Point, Seaview, Port Picky, Mermouth, Jinn and Tropicopacabanos came too, to make sure Serena wasn't wasting their money, and so did lots of parents from other towns who'd all been forced to give one of their children to the serpent. Acting on instructions from Serena, everyone had brought big bags of frozen pilchards and tins of sardines.

The boat got to Serpent Island just as the sun was going down. At first, all they could see were the waves slapping into the rock. Then Serena called out "Hello!" and the serpent's head slowly rose out of the water, his enormous eyes shut against the light.

"Stay there!" shouted Serena, in case the serpent came forward blindly and crashed into their boat. "Slowly lower your head and push it forward... a bit more... a bit to the left... Stop!"

The serpent stopped in front of the ship, his head just above the deck.

Quickly, Serena and her sisters unwrapped the package, revealing a giant pair of sunglasses with a big rubber strap instead of arms.

"We're going to put something on you now," explained Serena. "To help you see 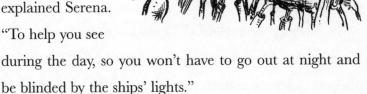 during the day, so you won't have to go out at night and be blinded by the ships' lights."

"I'm not sure I like this," complained the serpent, as the seventeen girls slipped the sunglasses on his head and tightened the strap around his horns.

"You'll get used to them," said Serena. "You can open your eyes now."

"Are you sure?" asked the serpent. Hesitantly he opened one eye a tiny bit. Then he opened it a bit more, then both his eyes flashed open as wide as they could go.

"I can see!" he explained. "I can see in the daytime!"

"They're polarising sunglasses," explained Serena, who of course knew everything there was to know about glasses of all kinds. "That means they change depending how sunny it is. When there's lots of light they get darker, but at night they will be almost clear, so you can see both day and night."

"Thank you," said the serpent. "This will certainly help me not to run into your ships. But I'm afraid it's come too late."

"What do you mean?" asked Serena. She thought she'd completely solved the problem. All that was left was to tie up the boat next to the rock, put a line of pilchards and sardines on the gangplank and lure the penguimaids aboard. Then when they dried out, they'd all be girls again.

"There's hardly any weed left anywhere," said the serpent sadly. "I must have taken too much to feed the penguimaids and myself, and the weed beds will take months to grow back. You can take the penguimaids back home, but I'm going to starve."

Chapter Twelve

A single tear emerged from the serpent's eye and slipped out under his new sunglasses. Everyone on the boat felt like crying too, because the serpent was so nice and he was being so brave.

"Can't you eat anything else?" asked Serena as her mighty brain tried to think of what they could possibly do.

"I'm a vegetarian," sniffed the serpent. "And there's only one sort of seaweed which has the vitamins and minerals that a growing sea serpent needs."

"Hmmm," said Serena. Then she turned around to everyone in the boat and said, "Has anyone brought salad for their lunch?"

Lots of people raised their hands. Soon Serena was going through their paper bags and lunch boxes, pulling out pieces of lettuce and cabbage and cucumber and rocket and cos and other salad stuff that only she knew the proper names for.

Piece by piece she fed these to the serpent, and piece by piece he spat them out.

"Yuck! No! Blah! Eck! Thpew!" he said, till finally Serena put a single long leaf of something dark green and crunchy on his tongue.

"Yum!" said the serpent. "That's got all the right stuff in it. What's that?"

"Spinach," said Serena. "I don't like it myself, but it seems to me that we can keep you going with lots of spinach, at least until the weed grows back."

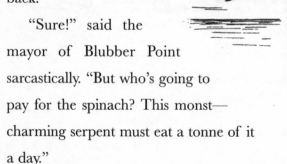

"Sure!" said the mayor of Blubber Point sarcastically. "But who's going to pay for the spinach? This monst— charming serpent must eat a tonne of it a day."

"We're not paying!" shouted all the other mayors. Now that the danger of the serpent running into shipping was gone, they didn't care about anything else. "Let's go!"

Chapter Thirteen

"Oh," said Serena, "I suppose you're not worried about a starving sea serpent coming ashore to look for spinach in town then? Slithering through the streets to the supermarket?"

The serpent – who was very honest – started to say something about not being able to go into shallow water, but Serena held up her hand.

"Sssshh," she said. "Can you imagine, Mayor? Just think what would happen if the serpent got into the fruit and vegetable department at Foodplanet?"

The mayor of Blubber Point frowned and groaned and pulled at her hair. But she knew there was no point arguing with Serena. She was always right! It was unbearable.

Finally the mayor looked at all the other mayors. They nodded.

"Oh, all right," she sighed. "We'll pay for daily deliveries of spinach until the seaweed grows back. We'll put it on the same rocks where we used to put out the children for the serpent."

"With floats, so it doesn't sink if it washes off," said Serena. "Now, we need to get the penguimaids aboard."

It took some time to get all the penguimaids on the boat. It was quite dark and everyone stank of pilchards and sardines by the time the black and white birds were all safely asleep down belowdecks, their flippers folded over their enormously fat stomachs.

Finally, Serena peered out into the darkness. She could just see the serpent's head because tonight there was no moon.

"Serpent, how much weed have you got left?" she asked quietly. "Enough to turn one person into a penguimaid?"

"Yes, I guess so," rumbled the serpent. "Why?"

"I want you to turn me back into one," Serena said, as softly as she could. But her sisters still heard her.

"What?" they all shrieked, and Suzy, Sally, Sapphira and Sappho rushed across and grabbed her left arm. Serendipity, Susan, Suky and Silvia grabbed her right arm.

Salome, Sheila, Sidonie and Sophie grabbed her left leg. Stella, Sigrid, Sonia and Stephanie grabbed her right leg. Then everyone fell over and got in a fearful tangle. Of course, Serena had somehow wriggled out while her sisters struggled on the deck.

"Only for a few weeks," she said crossly. "I get so tired of knowing everything and having to sort everything out. When I was a penguimaid I didn't have to think! I didn't have to be right! I just swam around and had fun! *I want a holiday!*"

"Good idea," said the mayor of Blubber Point.

"If you're sure," said the serpent.

"Absolutely," said Serena. She bent down to look at Suzy, whose face she could just see in a tangle of sisters.

"Come and get me in two weeks. And tell Mum and Dad not to worry. the serpent keeps sharks well away from the island."

Suzy nodded. On her third nod, Serena wasn't there any more. There was only a penguin, who scooped up a dropped sardine from the deck then jumped overboard.

A few minutes later, Serena waddled ashore and found a nice pebble-lined hole to curl up in. Soon she was asleep and her dreams were *not* about everything there was to know in fifty-seven encyclopaedias in twelve different languages.

She dreamed of shining fish and clear blue seas and underwater loop-the-loop, and slept so soundly she didn't wake until the serpent nudged her the next morning.

Straight away, Serena got up and dived into the sea – without a single thought.